SMOKY RANGE

E. E. Halleran was born in Wildwood, New Jersey. He graduated with a Bachelor's degree from Bucknell University in Lewisburg, Pennsylvania, and did postgraduate work at Temple University Law School, Rutgers University where he earned a Master's degree in Education, and the University of Pennsylvania in Philadelphia. He worked as a teacher of social studies at Ocean City High School in New Jersey from 1928 until his retirement in 1949. Halleran began publishing Western stories in magazines, with stories in Wild West, Western Story, and feature articles about Western American history in Big-Book Western. His first novel, *No Range is Free*, was published by Macrae Smith in 1944 and had both commercial and critical success. It was followed that same year by *Prairie Guns* (Macrae Smith, 1944). *Indian Fighter* (Ballantine, 1964) won a Spur Award as Best Western Historical Novel from the Western Writers of America. Halleran's Western fiction is meticulously researched with notable accuracy, both as to the period in which it is set and often populated by historical personalities, while the stories are filled with suspense and fast-paced drama. Among the characters in *Prairie Guns* are Wild Bill Hickok, while he was still a U. S. marshal, and the Indian chieftain Roman Nose. His characters, both fictitious and historical, appear against backdrops of documented historical events through which the historical characters actually lived, and without any overt attempt to create legends or myths. His descriptive and narrative talent is always such that a reader is instantly swept up by the events of the story and becomes deeply involved with the characters. Among his finest books—always a difficult choice with this author—are *No Range is Free*, *Outposts Of Vengeance* (Macrae Smith, 1945) set during the time of the war with the Miami Indians, and *Winter Ambush* (Macrae Smith, 1954) concerned with the attempt by the U. S. Army to quell a Mormon uprising.

SMOKY RANGE

E. E. Halleran

GUNSMOKE

First published in the UK by Hammond

This hardback edition 2012
by AudioGO Ltd
by arrangement with
Golden West Literary Agency

ISBN 978 1 445 85069 6

British Library Cataloguing in Publication Data available.

Printed and bound in Great Britain by
MPG Books Group Limited

Chapter One

THE FLIMSY WALLS of the Copper King Hotel were far from gas-proof. Even in cold weather, with all cracks plugged, they permitted smelter fumes to seep into the place until every battered chair carried its burden of copper grime and every bed sheet and blanket was impregnated with sulphur and arsenic. On a warm spring night, with rickety windows propped open, there was little to choose between Butte's smoke-laden exterior and its equally grimy interiors. The "Richest Hill on Earth" was bringing plenty of dollars into the former silver mining camp but it was also smothering the town in a fog of smelter gases which made even hardened old-timers strangle.

Young Doctor Burdick turned away from the open window where he had been staring down into the dimly lighted street, a frown puckering his angular features. From an open tin trunk he took a black leather bag, fondling it for just a moment before opening it to glance anxiously at the neatly packed instruments in their shining rows. With so much sulphur in the air he wouldn't have been surprised to find the metal beginning to tarnish even in the three short hours since he had descended from the Northern Pacific train. Three hours of inhaling those fumes gave a man that sort of feeling.

For just a moment the frown of distaste became a crooked smile, partly at sight of those cherished instruments and partly in scornful recognition of his own anxiety. Then he replaced the bag, locked the trunk, and went out. Experience with the Butte of an earlier day told him that there would be no point in locking the sagging door of the hotel room but that it would be sound common sense to lock the trunk. A young medico, just starting out in the world, could not afford to buy equipment for casual thieves to steal.

Out in the gloom of the street he strolled somewhat unhappily along past dingy but well-lighted stores, saloons, restaurants, and other commercial enterprises calculated to drain off a share of the city's mounting prosperity. Miners, smelter workers, teamsters, and assorted townsmen brushed past him, vague, hurrying shapes in the malodorous night. Five years ago, when silver had dominated Butte's economy, he would have known many citizens by name; tonight he was a stranger in a city which suddenly had become foreign to him, a nightmare town of grimy people in a fog of choking copper fumes through which even the steady rumble of the stamp mills seemed to come in muffled fashion.

Again the rueful smile tugged at the wide mouth as he recalled the bright plans he had been making during the past couple of years. The newspapers in Chicago had made much of the sudden growth of the copper town, and Frank Burdick had considered it almost as a personal invitation. What better break could a medical student ask than to find a familiar community growing so briskly? He had even considered, not entirely humorously, the obvious fact that copper smelters would not make for a healthy atmosphere. A doctor might do very well by himself in such a town.

A grim chuckle came from his throat at the memory. Butte had changed, all right, just as the papers had declared, but he couldn't imagine himself remaining in the town. A doctor might make a small fortune treating lung diseases but he would probably die of the same malady before he could enjoy his properly gained affluence.

Preoccupied by his own sense of disappointment he suddenly realized that he was approaching a little knot of idlers who had gathered around a street-corner hawker. From the vantage point of superior height Doctor Burdick could see the flaming torches which the peddler had raised on poles. Idly curious he moved closer, noting that the spieler was as tall a man as himself, a bustling young fellow with a broad grin and a line of good-humored patter calculated to put the prospective customers in a proper buying spirit.

"Seriously," the tall peddler was saying, dropping his elaborate air of banter, "not a man of you dares to be without it. Every moment of every day your lungs are assaulted by every corrosive gas known to man—and several not known to him. You breathe arsenic, sulphur, wood smoke, and gaseous copper all the time. Science knows no sure antidote for these poisons except other elements which would be instantly fatal if introduced into the human system. The only defense at our disposal is the marvelous healing powers of the human constitution. That's right, brother, even a miserable specimen of a human body like yours has those healing powers."

There was a laugh as the hawker poked fun at a little man in the front row. Burdick frowned professionally as he realized that he was listening to one of those medical fakers so despised by ethical members of the profession, but a sense of curiosity pulled him forward. It was something new to hear a quack open his show without claiming to have a cure for all of the world's evils—and it was almost as strange to see such a young man operating the graft. Usually it required quite a period of apprenticeship for a faker to acquire the aplomb necessary for the game but this fellow was perhaps a year or two younger than Burdick.

"Your lungs," the faker continued, "provide nature's own antidote, a natural product of the bloodstream known to the scientific world as anticuprousanodyne." He rattled off the term without blinking. "Every human body produces it in sufficient quantities to overcome ordinary gas inhalations. That's right, mister, even yours. But here in Butte no ordinary constitution is equipped to combat so much sulphur, so much arsenic, so much lead oxide and all the other effluvia incidental to the smelter business—and local politics. We have to help our natural recuperative powers, remarkable as they are. We have to supplement the natural supply of anticuprousanodyne with extra fortification— No, my friend, not the kind of fortification I detect on your breath."

He waited for his laugh with all the careful timing of an old hand, continuing: "That fortification, gentlemen, is what I'm introducing here this evening. I'm not asking you to pay the full value of this remarkable preparation. I'm not even asking you to meet the cost paid by me to the famous scientific laboratory which produces it. I'm practically giving you the trial size for one dollar."

He gestured expansively as the crowd hooted its skepticism. "Naturally I'm planning to make a profit out of this business, folks. Every man takes a profit if he expects to stay in business. I know that when you learn the amazing restorative qualities of this product you will become steady users—and by that time I'll be charging you the regular commercial price. You'll have to pay me full value if you hope to maintain your health and comfort in this vale of tears and foul odors. I'll get you then—but tonight you can take advantage of my method of advertising. The introductory offer lets you get ahead of the game. One dollar for the trial size. What can you lose? What's a dollar in Butte?"

Again Doctor Burdick's somewhat ascetic features alternated between a frown and a grin. As a newly fledged physician he was annoyed at this garrulous faker but at the same time he was amused by the man's glib exploitation of the town's unhappy plight. Other quacks had sold nostrums with similar spiels but this fellow was applying a certain amount of ingenuity to his fraud. Burdick remembered his own thoughts regarding Butte's unhealthy atmosphere as a source of potential revenue and chuckled aloud. Evidently the idea hadn't been his own exclusive property.

He watched while several roughly clad men pushed forward to purchase the gaudily labeled eight-ounce bottles, then he strode on along the street, trying to bring his thoughts back to the problem which confronted him. Very soon he would have to decide about that matter of setting up in practice and already he knew that his half-made choice of Butte would have to be changed. Regardless of prosperity prospects he didn't propose to settle here in this strangling valley.

He had not gone a hundred paces when a soft footstep sounded behind him and something hard pushed against his spine.

"Stand still!" a voice ordered harshly. "Get them hands up!"

Burdick obeyed, speaking quietly as he did so. "Sorry, friend, but I just naturally forgot to bring my pocketbook with me. It's practically empty, anyhow."

A hand was already making a hurried search of his person, finding nothing for the very good reason that Burdick had been guarding against just such a holdup attempt. It wasn't likely that Butte's manners had improved much in the past five years so he had locked his money in the tin trunk.

"Don't git gay!" the bandit warned, the gun jabbing angrily into the muscles of Burdick's back. "I want money, not gab."

Burdick tried again, edging away from the prodding gun muzzle. "I'm just telling you," he said mildly. "I'm not joking; I'm stony. Lend me a gun and I might even go into partnership with you."

The humor didn't get quite the result Burdick had anticipated. The pressure of the gun suddenly relaxed but only because the bandit had swung the weapon as a club, crashing down on the side of Burdick's head.

"That's fer tryin' to be funny!" the voice snarled. "And next time yuh better carry some dinero wit' yuh!" It was a parting salute, the thug's voice fading away with final phrase.

Burdick held steady until retreating footsteps in a side alley assured him that the footpad had fled. Then he turned to stare into the darkness where his assailant had disappeared, commenting audibly as he rubbed the lump which was beginning to swell over his ear. "Looks like everybody's trying to help me make up my mind—to go somewhere else."

In the next twenty minutes he watched two energetic fights between Irish and Cornish miners, ducked into a doorway to avoid the wild bullets of a brief but deadly gun battle, and was twice accosted by hoarse-voiced women of the line who cursed him when he responded with flat negatives. Finally he turned back toward the Copper King, his last lingering doubts dispersed. Tomorrow he would take the stage for Osage to visit Uncle Jeff. After that he would have to start planning all over again. Butte might be a prosperous community but its flavor was a trifle too strong for a man who was a little proud of a new dignity and respectability. Butte, the silver camp, had been a good town for the celebrations of Frank Burdick, cowboy, but Butte, the copper capital, was no place for Frank Burdick, M.D.

On the return walk he dodged one saloon brawl, eventually coming to the corner where the hawker had been selling his nostrums. The neighborhood was quite dark now but just ahead of him Burdick could see a long-legged man carrying a small bundle. He had a hunch that it was the quack but before he could verify his guess there was a second shadow in the gloom ahead, a bulkier form which had emerged suddenly from a lane to close in on the tall faker. Burdick didn't need to be told that here was another holdup attempt.

Somewhat to his own surprise he found himself hurrying forward, moving as noiselessly as possible on the soft, moist earth. A now familiar harsh voice was ordering, "Get 'em up, Doc! I know yuh got some sucker dollars in yuhr pocket—and wit' me sucker money is as good as any." There was no mistaking the voice. Burdick let one hand stray to the knob over his ear as he closed in on the stocky thief's back.

For the moment it did not seem at all incongruous that a reputable medical man should be going into violent action in defense of a blatant medical faker. Actually Doctor Burdick didn't even consider the point. All he knew

was that the thug ahead of him was the same surly bandit
who had banged him on the head for no reason except ill
nature over a feeble bit of whimsy. That blow deserved a
retort, and Frank Burdick was just the man to do the re-
torting, medical diploma or no medical diploma.

He launched himself in a driving charge just as the
surprised thug took the alarm and half turned to meet the
attack. Burdick missed his grip but the force of his lunge
upset the stocky man, throwing him into the hawker so
that all three of them went down in a flailing tangle of
arms and legs. Burdick drove home one solid punch, then
concentrated on getting hold of the bandit's gun.

For several frantic moments he didn't know whether he
was wrestling with the right man or not but then a rake
of metal along one cheekbone offered painful reassurance
on the point. The blow staggered him but also stung him
into more determined effort. One long hand closed over
the cold metal of a gun barrel just as the other hand
clamped down on the thick wrist behind the gun. At the
same instant there was the thud of a fist meeting flesh but
Burdick did not wait to learn who was hitting whom. He
simply braced his feet under him in a half-crouch, twisting
so as to get shoulder leverage under the captured arm.
After that he moved with all the well-learned skill of yes-
teryear. There was a grunt as the stocky man was flailed
over that straining shoulder, then a combination of thud
and grunt as the outlaw struck the ground.

Instantly the peddler flung himself past Burdick, div-
ing at the fallen thief. Almost as promptly he rolled clear
and stood erect in the gloom. "Out cold," he announced
with complete calm but some lack of breath. "A very neat
trick, brother, and thanks. You didn't break his damned
neck, did you—I hope?"

Burdick fingered the gun which had come loose to remain in his grasp. "Probably not," he replied, breathing
a little heavily. "How about you? Are you hurt?"

"Nope. I'm righter'n rain in a parched and weary land.
But let's you and me get outa here. A man never knows

how the law dogs are goin' to bark in this stink hole of perdition. That jasper might even be a worthy deputy marshal makin' up a few deficits in his modest income. Let's make tracks."

Doctor Burdick didn't resist as the peddler urged him along down the street. Regardless of how his future plans might work out there was no point in staying around to be identified with a street brawl. People might misunderstand. Some of the old-timers might even remember young Frank Burdick of Diamond K and think he hadn't changed much. That wouldn't be good advertising for the new Frank Burdick.

He jammed the gun into his waistband, quite unconscious of the ease with which the gesture came back to him, his lips a little tight as he strode along beside his companion. Then the tightness relaxed, and he grinned again, half amused at his own concern. He had been disturbed over becoming identified with a street fight but he was carelessly proposing to appear in public with a hawker of fake medicines. That wouldn't be good business, either, but enough of the Diamond K Burdick was in him so that suddenly he didn't care.

Somewhat to Burdick's surprise his companion led him straight back to the Copper King Hotel, talking volubly every step of the way. It was clear that the fellow was still highly excited over the brush with the outlaw and more than a little embarrassed over his debt of gratitude to a stranger.

"Come up and get the blood off your phiz," the hawker invited as they approached the rickety inn. "I've got bunk room in the loft of this flea trap."

Burdick had forgotten the blow he had taken in the first part of the fight but now a quick hand came away from his cheek showing a smear of blood. He grimaced a little as he followed the other man through a knot of staring loungers, the gesture both an expression of annoyance at his own injury and of brief amusement at the hawker's derisive reference to the Copper King's vaunted second story.

Neither of them spoke again until they were in the bare hallway above, groping through the Stygian darkness. Then Burdick remarked, "I guess we're neighbors. My room is right here somewhere."

"Yeah? Then you must be the jasper who blew into town on the Montana Union this afternoon. I saw you arriving."

"Montana— Oh, I remember. That's the local name of the Northern Pacific spur line, isn't it? Correct. I arrived on it."

"Welcome to our stinkin' city. I'm practically an old resident. Been here three days." He shoved open a door as he added, "Come along and I'll see if I can't patch you up a bit."

Burdick halted in the darkness, professional resentment coming back to him. "You mean you're a surgeon as well as a maker of healing miracles?"

The other man laughed, evidently not hearing the note of irony in the question. "So you witnessed the Dillingham pitch, did you? Every feller to his own graft, you know."

"Graft?"

"Sure. Between friends I don't mind admitting that it's just a little harmless fun with the local yokels. Gold bricks are a better line but out here there's too much real gold for the trade article to be in much demand. So I became Doctor C. C. Dillingham and offered the assembled citizenry a lung cure."

He was fumbling for a lamp as he spoke. Burdick stopped in the doorway, still trying to summon an outraged dignity but not having too much luck with it. "Then the cure is just a fake?"

"Sure. I might as well admit it. You'd know the truth anyway as soon as you took a gander at the Dillingham laboratory. But don't let it worry you. I can clean up that scratch for you as well as the next man."

He managed to put a match to the bracket lamp over

the unpromising-looking cot, a feeble yellow glow disclosing a remarkable set of medical properties on the floor in one corner. There was a gallon jug of unlabeled whisky, a partly filled box of unused eight-ounce bottles, a bundle of gummed labels, some corks, and two larger bottles of dark liquid.

"There she is," he said, gesturing airily. "The Dillingham laboratory."

For the first time Burdick realized that the man was of much the same physical description as himself. If he lacked a fraction of an inch of Burdick's six-foot-two he made up for it with an extra pound of well-proportioned shoulder. Also like Burdick he was inclined to be angular of feature, the angularity relieved by a show of humor that might have been merely professional geniality but which seemed like a natural quality.

Burdick found it hard to avoid the infectiousness of the other's grin. It was annoying to find himself forced into such obvious comparison with a medical quack but he still couldn't put the proper severity into his voice when he announced, "I am Doctor Frank Burdick."

Dillingham faltered for just an instant. "You mean a real M.D.?"

"Yes."

"Gosh! I didn't even guess. Well, every man to his own graft. I'd still like to help you clean up that scrape—acting as a plain citizen, of course, with no medical license."

The grinning impudence was completely inoffensive, and Burdick smiled. "I guess I can take care of it myself, thanks. I appreciate the good will, though."

"Have it your own way. Slip out of that coat while I get some water and we'll see if it's much of a slash. By the way, the C. C. in my name is real. It stands for Christopher Columbus and my friends—when and if I happen to find any —call me Lum."

In spite of the brisk air there was a wistfulness in the remark which caught Burdick's sympathy. "All right, Lum," he said, smiling briefly. "Let me take a look at myself in that regal mirror the hotel supplied you with."

The words seemed to establish a quick bond between them and for the next few minutes they joked easily while Burdick attended to his own injury. It proved to be only a scratch so after cleaning it out well he let it alone, deciding that he would take better care of it later.

"Have a drink?" Dillingham inquired.

Burdick glanced at the jug. "No, thanks."

Dillingham interpreted his glance and reached under the cot for a flask. "This is the drinkin' liquor," he confided with a wink. "That stuff in the jug is medicine. Whisky, water, and a little mixture of flavors. That's my formula. Not enough of anything to hurt anybody but enough alcohol to tickle the gullet. Great stuff!"

Burdick's lips tightened. "To kill people! They think they're getting treatment so they neglect the proper precautions. I wonder how many poor fools you've killed that way?"

Dillingham shrugged. "Let's not talk shop, Doc. I know you diploma boys ain't got much time for us spielers but don't hold it against me now. Have a drink."

"Sorry. I don't believe a physician should addle his brains with alcohol." There was a little trace of stiffness in the statement but Dillingham met it with the same grin.

I don't drink, either," he replied. "And for the same reason. When a man lives by his wits he needs 'em razor-sharp all the time. I just keep the liquor for friends—or customers."

Burdick managed a smile but moved toward the door. It was all well and good to be amused by an odd character like Lum Dillingham but there was still the matter of professional ethics to be considered. Better to break off the interview before any further fraudulent confidences could be offered.

As he turned, however, his eye caught a headline in the crumpled newspaper which lay on a corner of the washstand. It was the *Butte Miner*, a violently partisan sheet which Uncle Jeff had occasionally sent him during the first years of his student career. He recognized the style, mostly a series of graduated headlines which managed to tell the bulk of the story before ever getting down to the details in small print. For the most part the paper dealt with local tales of violence, either the physical riotousness of the town's rugged career or the oral violence engendered by the bitter fight between Clark's mining interests and the Anaconda outfit of Marcus Daly.

"No news there," Dillingham commented, noting the start of surprise. "That rag's two weeks old. It's the wrapper the saloon man used for my jug of laboratory liquor."

Burdick did not reply. Almost in a daze he was reading the article which had caught his attention, an article whose headlines read:

PROMINENT BIG HOLE BASIN MAN MURDERED

*Jefferson Burdick, Banker, Cattleman, and Stage Line
Owner, Found Dead in His Office at Osage.
Sheriff Tex Hickey Believes Killing Is Connected
with Violent Tactics of Mining Interests.*

He controlled himself to ask quietly, "Do you mind if I take this along with me?"

Dillingham stared. "Help yourself. But what's—"

There was no reply. Burdick was out in the gloom of the hallway, fumbling for his own door. Uncle Jeff dead! Murdered! But why? And the time. A full two weeks ago. Why had there been no notification?

Chapter Two

IT SEEMED LIKE HOURS to Burdick before he could get the lamp lighted in his own room. Then an almost professional calm took the place of the numbness, and he began to study the crumpled paper. It was just two weeks old, the murder story having been three days old when printed.

Burdick made a swift calculation. He had not left Chicago until fully a week after the tragedy. The telegraph was swift enough between Butte and Chicago and the news had been in Butte early enough to be in this paper. There must have been from five to seven days in which he should have received word of his uncle's death. Why hadn't that word arrived?

He read the article again, learning nothing new. There was simply the flat statement that Jefferson Burdick had been mysteriously killed, dying instantly from a gunshot wound in the temple. The rest of the article was devoted to an account of the many enterprises in which the dead man had been interested. A final paragraph mentioned the exploits of the Burdick brothers in the early days of the Big Hole Basin, noting that the only surviving member of the family was a nephew now somewhere in the East. No hint as to the cause of the murder was offered, nothing to follow up the headline's hint.

Suddenly Burdick dropped the paper and went out of the room, the scratch on his cheek forgotten. Again men looked curiously at him as he went through the open front door of the hotel, but he scarcely saw them. Taking the long strides natural to him he hurried along downgrade toward the spot where the Big Hole Transportation Company had maintained its stage and freight station. He had intended to look it up next day but now he knew that another part of his program would have to be altered.

The town had changed considerably in that quarter but he found the unpainted stage station much as it had been five years previously. In the gloom behind it he fancied that he could see a somewhat larger stable and warehouse than had been there earlier but the office was the same, a yellow lamplight shining through windows which were only a little dirtier than they had been in the old days. That much he saw even through the riot of thoughts which had been running through his mind. It was still difficult to believe that sturdy old Uncle Jeff was dead but the realization was beginning to strike home, bringing with it all the wild conjectures suggested by the murder story.

He went in swiftly, causing a sudden movement on the part of the two men who had been sitting at a table in a far corner behind the plank barrier. One of them was small and almost dapper while the other was roughly clad, a squat, swarthy man whose bulk seemed out of proportion to his short, heavy frame. Neither man was at all familiar to Doctor Burdick.

"Anything I can do for you, mister?" the dapper one inquired, leaving his companion.

"Are you the stage line agent?"

"I sure am."

"When's the first stage to Osage?"

"The usual time. Eight o'clock in the mornin'."

"Save me a ticket."

The agent smiled, disclosing a pair of missing teeth which somewhat spoiled his attempt at suavity. "No trouble on that score. The line ain't overcrowded since we've been limited to local trade. The Utah Northern grabs all the through passengers. Most days we only run as far as Osage."

"That's all right with me."

"Good. Have your luggage here by seven-forty." He moved across to the end of the counter and reached for a small ledger book. "Better leave your name, mister."

"I'm Doctor Frank Burdick."

"Doctor— Who? You mean you're—"

Burdick was conscious of the quick glance exchanged between the agent and the silent man at the table. It was a glance which hinted at something he could not understand but it drove him to an alertness which was reminiscent of the old days on the range. He had once felt that he had a nose for danger and now he was experiencing the familiar hunch that something was wrong.

"I am the nephew of Jefferson Burdick," he said clearly. "Did my uncle still own this company at the time of his death?"

Again there was an exchange of glances. Then the agent came around the barrier, extending a smooth white hand to Burdick. "I'm in charge here, Doctor. My name is Gregory Lane. I suppose it's useless to mention that we have all been pretty badly cut up over your uncle's untimely death. He still owned the line, along with half the other businesses in the basin. We're all wondering what's going to happen to our jobs now that he's gone."

Burdick ignored the sudden show of polish. "Who killed him?" he asked, the question as harsh as it was abrupt.

Lane shrugged narrow shoulders. "They can't seem to find out. I don't think this man Hickey is much of a detective."

Burdick relaxed a little, almost smiling as he replied, "I *know* he isn't. Beaver Head County elected him because he was tough not because he was any fellow for real brain work. But aren't there any clues at all?"

"Nothing definite. Your uncle had enemies, of course, just as any man with interests in so many deals would have. But there doesn't seem to be any real reason to accuse any of his business rivals."

"What about the article I noticed in the local paper? They hint that the Anaconda people might be responsible."

Lane laughed aloud, but it was the man in the corner who growled, "That's jest talk. Anyt'ing that goes wrong between Denver and Portland gits loaded onto the Daly gang by the Clark crowd. It don't mean a t'ing."

"That's right." Lane chuckled. "If you'll dig up a copy of the *Anaconda Standard* you'll likely find them pointing to your uncle's murder as some deep plot from the brain of W. A. Clark."

For a full minute Burdick didn't reply. Vaguely he realized that the Clark-Daly feud was being honestly appraised for him but the point did not seem important. The significant item was the gruff tones of the man in the far corner. That faintly Eastern accent, suggesting one of the seaboard cities—sounded remarkably familiar. It reminded him of a gun being hammered against the side of his head.

"Thanks," he said finally, turning away. "I'll be taking the stage in the morning."

He went out, still trying to stifle the sense of loss so that he might think clearly. Evidently there were a number of changes in plan that he would have to make. For the present the choice of location as a practicing physician might be the least important of these.

Fifty yards up the dark street he halted, trying to clear his mind. In that instant he heard a sound behind him that was distinct from the steady rumble of the stamp mills. It was the careful closing of a door which refused to perform silently. Wheeling to look back he was just in time to see the outline of a stocky figure crossing the street from the stage station. Seeing the man thus silhouetted Burdick knew that he had not been wrong about the voice. The burly man who had been on such confidential terms with Agent Lane was the street bandit who had so recently been defeated in his holdup attempt. The fact gave Burdick still another puzzle for his already confused thoughts.

Back at the Copper King he forced himself to calmness by treating the cut on his cheek. It wasn't much of a wound but the very business of smearing a bit of salve on it helped him to regain his poise. He was just completing the chore when there was a knock at the door and Dillingham came in.

"Hope I'm not bein' a nuisance, Doc," the hawker greeted, "but I had a hunch somethin' was wrong with you. I'd like to help—if you'll let me." He seemed to have lost some of his breeziness, his manner hinting that he felt a debt of gratitude and honestly wanted to repay it.

"Thanks," Burdick told him, "but there's nothing you can do. That paper of yours carried a story about a murder. It was my uncle who was murdered. The part that floored me is that I'd never been notified."

"Oh. Sorry to hear it." There was a pause before he added, "I didn't know but what you were a stranger in these parts."

"Hardly that. I lived around here all my life until I

went East to study medicine."

The word seemed to drive Dillingham to safer ground. He wanted to be friendly and he seemed to realize that the professional topic was not likely to be a congenial one. Suddenly he pointed to the six-gun which was still tucked in Burdick's belt. "What kind of a cannon did you take from that chump, Doc? Looks like a big one." He reached out as though to take the weapon but Burdick swept one hand across in a swift movement, the gun coming up so fast that Dillingham gasped aloud to find himself staring into the muzzle.

Burdick chuckled, amused at the other's reaction yet a little embarrassed at his own move. He had not intended to display the old skill of which he had once been so proud; it had just happened, quite without any thought on his part.

"Let me give you a piece of advice," he said, trying to cover his own confusion. "Don't reach for a man's gun in this country; he might misunderstand your motives." Then he reversed the weapon and handed it over.

Dillingham was still staring. "Holy smoke! You ain't the sober citizen I figured you for, Doc. How did you get that gun out so doggone fast?"

Burdick shrugged. "I practiced that move a lot longer than I practiced dissection. Maybe I'm a little rusty but—"

"Rusty! Brother, I've seen card sharper's fingers and I've watched many a shell game but I never saw anything as fast as that." He turned the .45 over gingerly. "What kind of a smoke pipe do you call this? I'm kinda ignorant about guns, being as it's right inconvenient to be caught carrying one when some nosy local cop hauls me off to the pokey for selling without a license. In my graft it's safer to be a poor innocent."

"It's a Colt forty-five," Burdick told him. "The usual thing in this country. Probably thousands of them in this state alone."

"Pretty good gun, huh?"

"The best."

"Then I guess we did all right tonight. Never go broke taking a profit, even if it pays off in hardware."

He handed the weapon back, and Burdick examined it for the first time, noting that it carried the usual load, all chambers full except the one under the hammer. It was clean but slightly battered, its cedar butt showing a variety of scratches as well as a rudely carved K inside of a somewhat lopsided diamond.

"That's odd," Burdick murmured. "This gun once belonged to somebody in my old outfit. That's our brand." He pointed to the Diamond K.

"You mean you could track down the bandit from this gun?"

"Not likely. Diamond K still operates and has been operating for a good many years. There must have been a hundred cowboys employed by the spread at one time or another and any one of them could have scratched that mark. It just struck me funny that I should have been held up by a gun from my old outfit." In the back of his mind he was considering a somewhat more notable coincidence but he didn't think it good policy to explain to a man like C. C. Dillingham. Confidences with confidence men were scarcely to be recommended.

Actually he didn't have time to talk any more. *"You* were held up?" Dillingham exclaimed. "I thought you just jumped in when the gun was on me."

Burdick remembered then that he had not even mentioned the first holdup of the evening. It was a subject to keep him clear of more personal matters so he kept the conversation there until Dillingham retreated to his own quarters, obviously impressed.

Only then did Burdick try to concentrate on the perplexing situation in which he had suddenly found himself. He sat in the darkness by the window, his mind gradually piecing out a pattern of memories which became a picture of the Big Hole Basin. There were plenty of gaps in the picture after a five-year absence but Burdick realized that he would have to provide himself with some sort of basis for the questions he proposed to search out. Somehow he had to get the facts about Uncle Jeff's death. Secondly he wanted to know why the tragedy had been kept secret from him. Maybe there was even a connection between the two questions.

Somewhat less definitely he had a feeling that the stocky street bandit must fit into the jigsaw puzzle somewhere. It wouldn't have been too great a coincidence to find a former Diamond K man turning thief but that familiarity between the thug and the stage agent hinted at a different conclusion. For some minutes Doctor Burdick even toyed with the idea that the original attack had been a personal one rather than an actual attempt at robbery. Then he put the thought aside. It seemed pretty certain that his identification of himself at the stage station had been a complete surprise to both men there. Also, the stocky man had attempted a similar holdup of Dillingham.

Gradually the lights of the town winked out as his mind struggled with the seemingly endless conjectures. Voices from the streets died away, and presently there was only the stench of sulphur and the distant rumble of stamps working around the clock. Finally Burdick moved across toward his cot, determined to push the whole thing out of his mind and get some sleep.

It was easier determined than accomplished. He was still wide awake when he heard the scrape of a shoe sole on the bare stairway. It brought him to instant alertness. The hotel had been completely quiet for more than an hour. A prowler out there now suggested trouble.

Twice more the sound came faintly to his ears, higher on the stairway each time. He eased out of bed, momentary tension broken as the sounds reminded him of the old child-scarer story about "Now I'm on the first step— Now I'm on the second step, etc." He smiled faintly at his own thoughts, suddenly aware that a different sound had come to his ears. Through the thin walls of the room he had heard the creak of a sagging cot spring. Dillingham was getting up. Evidently the talkative one was also awake and listening. Maybe he had even been waiting for this newcomer.

There was flat silence for what seemed like hours, only the subdued rumble of the stamps coming to straining ears. Burdick had a notion that the man in the hall had heard Dillingham and was waiting to find out what the move meant. In which case he was no partner of the hawker. Somehow that made Burdick feel better. He had begun to like the cheerful fraud and he didn't want to feel that the liking had been misplaced.

Then the footsteps sounded stealthily once more, coming along the hall. Burdick reached out to pick up the captured Colt, moving silently to a post near the door as soon as he was armed. There he waited until he heard the intruder fumbling at the flimsy latch of the door. For a second or two the faint rasp of metal was the only sound in the building but then there came an interruption as Dillingham's feet beat a sudden tattoo. The peddler was rushing into the hall, no longer trying to hide his own movements.

Almost at the same instant Burdick's door flew open and the room rocked under the impact of two explosions. The intruder had reached in to fire twice in the general direction of the cot. At least the flashes of the gun seemed aimed that way. Then the man was retreating.

It all happened so suddenly that Burdick couldn't make a move until it was over. Then he lunged in pursuit, aware that Dillingham and the gunman had already collided in the hall. There was a strangled curse and a thud of blows, but as he sprang forward the sounds receded downward. Snarling voices and thudding bodies told him that the battlers were rolling down the stairway, heads and heels banging the woodwork as they drummed their way down.

The hotel came to life with a roar but it was some minutes before anyone could bring a lamp. By that time the night prowler had dashed out into the darkness of the street, the light disclosing only the disgruntled Dillingham sprawled at the foot of the stairs. The man's nose was bleeding and he was holding a hand to his jaw, but generally the picture was one of grim comedy. Christopher Columbus Dillingham in his underwear was scarcely the jaunty figure of the street corner.

Burdick, gun in hand, found himself the center of a certain amount of suspicious attention but Dillingham shook off his grogginess to tell his story with some of his regular aplomb. A committee of undressed lodgers listened solemnly, then climbed the stairs for a look into Burdick's room. They swore politely at sight of a ragged hole in Burdick's mattress and at a second bullet hole in the outer wall, a hole made by a slug which must have barely missed the lumpy pillow on the cot. Then they went back to their own bunks, evidently not too much interested in the fact that someone had tried to murder a lodger. Perhaps most of the violent deaths in Butte did not take place quite so stealthily but any kind of death was too commonplace for men to lose much sleep over it.

When the last man had departed Burdick stared quizzically at his neighbor, noting that Dillingham was still holding a hand to his nose. "Want me to look at the injuries?" he inquired. "Or do you have an adequate nostrum for bloody noses?"

"Don't be so dam' humorous!" Dillingham growled. "This wasn't any joke."

"So I gather. My nasty sense of humor just happened to be tickled. Let me look you over. No charge, of course. I'm really quite grateful that you took the trouble to look after me."

Dillingham grinned past the bloody hand. "Maybe I oughta spend more time lookin' after myself. Two slugging jobs in one night is too much." He crossed to the scarred washstand and began to mop away some of the blood.

Burdick went over to help, stopping the nosebleed and treating the ugly lump that was beginning to swell on Dillingham's cheekbone. As he worked he talked, telling of his own precautions at hearing the intruder.

"I wondered," Dillingham said simply. "It looked to me like that one slug woulda got anybody lyin' on the cot."

"Likely. The jigger must have been a good shot, considering the way he blazed away in a hurry with no more light than was in this room."

"But who wants to kill you?"

"I don't know. I'd like to know who tried."

"Sorry. I never got any kind of a look at the skunk. I was too busy dodgin' fists and stair treads."

"Then you have no idea what sort of person he was?"

"Sure I do. He was tough!" He grinned ruefully and added, "At a guess I'd figure him to be a short, heavy man. That was the feeling I had when we were slugging it out with each other on the stairs."

"Short and heavy, eh? Like the bandit on the street?"

"Just about. Say! You don't suppose that rascal trailed us here and tried to get his gun back, do you?"

Burdick shook his head. "No. This man wasn't hunting any gun. He shot first—and without doing any amount of looking. He came here for only one purpose—to kill me."

"Why?"

"If I could answer that I'd know a lot about a number of questions that have been bothering me tonight. Well, that's patched up pretty well. Feel any better?"

Dillingham took the hint, drifting out after a few banal remarks. It left Burdick to do some more thinking, his perplexity flavored now with a sense of personal danger. No matter what had been behind the holdup attempt on the street this last incident had been attempted murder and nothing else. He could only guess that there was a connection between that attempt and the murder of Uncle Jeff.

Chapter Three

HE WAS STILL TRYING to find a clue to the puzzle when he started for the stage line office next morning. Ahead of him the Copper King's grizzled swamper trundled the tin trunk on a wheelbarrow, but Burdick paid him little heed. Almost for the first time since the neat letters had been painted on the lacquered metal he was not taking any pride in the *Frank L. Burdick, M.D.* There were too many other matters to claim his attention. After last night's events he knew that he had to be alert for trouble every minute. Certainly that last attack had been warning enough.

An old but neatly painted Concord stood in the lane beside the office, its boot already half filled with boxes and trunks. Two men in flannel shirts and miner's boots were talking with Lane while a dark-haired young woman in a brown traveling-gown stood back against the wall, staring fixedly at nothing. Burdick saw that she was pretty in spite of her look of complete severity, but there was no opportunity for him to give her the attention she deserved. Lane, the stage line agent, was coming to greet him, suddenly very gracious as though realizing that this lanky young man with the grim jaw was his new boss. Or there might be another reason for the graciousness, Burdick decided, recalling the way Lane had been so familiar with that stocky gunman.

"Sorry I didn't wake up last evening, Doctor," Lane greeted. "You were gone before I could quite realize that it was actually you."

Burdick's face was expressionless. "No harm done. I was as rattled as anyone else. I had just learned of my uncle's death. Saw it by chance in an old paper."

"You mentioned that point. I didn't understand until later. Then I began to wonder why you didn't know before."

"It's a point that's been bothering me. I never received any notice."

Lane's frown seemed genuine. "That's sure an odd one. Sorry I can't give you any more information than I did last night. The whole thing's a big mystery, I understand."

Burdick decided that the man was either honest or an excellent actor. In either case there seemed to be no profit in trying any pumping tactics. He changed the subject abruptly. "Do I buy my ticket from you or the driver?"

Lane grinned. "Neither. I don't think the line will be interested in taking your money." He made it sound like a confidential joke between them. "Where's your luggage?"

Burdick motioned toward the man with the barrow, and Lane bustled away, issuing crisp orders to the stablemen who were doubling as porters. Then he spoke in a low voice to the tall, wiry man who had already mounted to the driver's seat. Burdick heard the driver referred to as Slats but he could not recall him as anyone he had known in the old days. Evidently the stage line had undergone quite a few changes in personnel during the past five years.

A couple of men loaded the tin trunk in on top of the other boxes, Burdick paying off the barrowman meanwhile. It was only as the shambling swamper started away that Burdick noticed the tall man hurrying down the hill from the direction of the Copper King. It was C. C. Dillingham and he was carrying a newspaper-wrapped bundle under one arm. Judging by his haste he was intending to take passage on the stagecoach.

Burdick frowned briefly at the prospect of the faker's company but the frown was just a gesture. Dillingham was a hard man to despise, no matter what his ethics might be. Burdick even found himself a little sympathetic at sight of the bundle. It was probably just a lot of empty bottles wrapped up in an extra shirt. Certainly Dillingham hadn't been enjoying too much prosperity with his medicine graft.

The peddler winked once as he approached but did not speak to Burdick, going directly into the stage office to arrange for passage. After that he came out and shoved his rope-tied bundle into the boot. That done he seemed to regain some of his breezy self-confidence. At any rate he sidled toward the dark-haired girl, greeting her with a marked deference which almost concealed his nerve in making the approach. She did not even glance at him but continued to stare into the distance just as she had been doing ever since Burdick's arrival. Dillingham grinned at the rebuff, then strolled on across toward Burdick.

"Respectable," he announced, not bothering to lower his voice. "Won't speak to me." The pronouncement of judgment answered a question which had been in Burdick's mind.

"Decided to move on?" he asked idly.

Dillingham nodded. "Yep. Somehow this copper-poison spiel didn't hit folks like I figured it would—and it's too hard keeping your profits in this town. Too many gents with guns anxious to declare themselves a dividend. I had a hunch I'd give Salt Lake City a try."

"Then you'd better take the railroad. This stage line's local."

"I know. But that's the way I have to handle it. Short hops with a bit of business along the way. Got to make expenses, you know."

Again Burdick knew a sense of irritation that he should be in the confidence of a fellow like Dillingham but he decided not to make any fuss about it. Instead he commented, "You'll have to change the game. Butte's poisonous atmosphere is limited, you know."

"That's the beauty of my kind of medicine," the other told him with a wink. "In the cow country it'll be just a spring tonic and when I get to Salt Lake I'll switch labels again."

Burdick laughed in spite of himself. "Were you figuring the Mormons to be particularly health-conscious—or just extra foolish?"

Dillingham winked again. "I kinda figured I'd try the salt game on 'em."

"What's the salt game?"

"Just another on-the-spot invention from the fertile brain of C. C. Dillingham, at your service. Too much salt in the system is supposed to cause high blood pressure, isn't it?"

"Some authorities hold to that theory."

"There you are. Folks in Utah live in an atmosphere of salt. I'll sell 'em my little panacea as a tonic for relieving the overbalance of salt. Mormons oughta snap it up. With all them wives they've got too much blood pressure in the first place."

There was no time for further talk—not that any was needed. Lane called for passengers to take their seats, and Burdick watched interestedly as one of the miners climbed to the box with the gaunt driver while the other clambered into the coach. Lane scowled as the man brushed by him, then became all smiles as he helped the girl in. Dillingham went next, taking the seat beside the girl, and leaving Burdick to take the opposite corner. The arrangement suited Burdick well enough; he had been chiefly concerned with estimating the character of his fellow passengers, remembering the danger which certainly surrounded him. Now he decided that the two mining men did not know each other but that the one in the vacant guard seat on the box might be the man to watch. It was only a guess, but when a man was threatened he had to be making all sorts of guesses.

Dillingham started to talk immediately, offering a running fire of humorous comment as the stage labored up the grade out of the bowl in which the town was located. For the most part he was genially critical of the town they were leaving, an attitude which seemed entirely acceptable to both the girl and the miner. Within the first quarter hour he had broken down formal restraints and the girl was smiling pleasantly enough at his whimsy while the bearded man's grumbling comments were almost agreeable in spite of their tone. Burdick remained silent, studying the two strangers covertly while appearing to be aloof and disinterested.

He concluded that the miner was a rather sour type of individual but not one of any particular interest. There was nothing in his speech or attitude to even hint that he might be concerned with the mysterious attacks upon Frank Burdick or with the murder of Jefferson Burdick.

Maybe it was a little ridiculous even to consider the point but there would be no relaxing of suspicion until a lot of questions were answered.

So far as the girl was concerned Burdick was simply interested. Seeing her now at close quarters he realized that his first impression had not done her justice. Her features were good, a little too regular to be lively but with a slight roundness that hinted at warmth rather than classic beauty. Her complexion was a smooth tan and her dark, wavy hair formed a striking background for eyes that were almost a perfect turquoise-blue. Like her face her figure was pleasantly rounded, drawing attention away from the fact that her height was somewhat above average. It was obvious that Dillingham was properly appreciative of her charms. As soon as she offered her first answering smile he stopped talking for the benefit of the two men and concentrated on keeping her entertained.

Once she looked up and caught Burdick's eye, her smile hinting that she was amused by the voluble fellow at her side and was willing to share that amusement with a fellow traveler. At least Burdick had a feeling that he understood her to that degree. She did not look toward him again, however, and he let his attention wander to the bright morning outside. The coach was still climbing the steep grades of the mountains west of the town, and Burdick let his memory drift back to the other times when he had ridden this trail, usually with other young fellows from the cattle spreads of the Big Hole country. The trail had been a bit rougher in those days but the air certainly had been better. Even up here he could still smell the fumes of sulphur.

The night's loss of sleep began to tell on him as his thoughts wandered and presently he dropped into a doze, awakening only when the coach struck the downgrades beyond the divide. Its speed increased then, and the four passengers held on grimly, taking their jolting in silence while the brakes howled a noisy protest. Then they were rolling along an easier trail, following the Big Hole River.

Burdick promptly went to sleep again. That trick of taking cat naps was at least one old habit that fitted well with his new life as a medical man.

When he awoke again they were grinding to a halt at Fishtrap. To most passengers Fishtrap meant a quick meal and a brief stretch while the team was being changed. To Burdick it meant a renewal of his alertness. Until he knew what was going on in the basin he had to watch everybody.

The brief halt gave him no grounds for suspicion, however. Dillingham paid strict attention to the dark-haired girl. The two miners ate without paying any attention to anyone, including each other. Slats, the driver, stuck strictly to business, speaking to his passengers only when it was time for them to get back in the coach. Burdick was interested to note that he called the girl Miss Lowry, his tone carrying a ring of respect. Otherwise the only noteworthy point was the way everyone ignored Burdick's identity. Under the circumstances the stage line employees might have been expected to make some effort to greet a probable new boss but they didn't even look at him. He was forced to the conclusion that Lane hadn't identified him to the driver. Apparently no one but Dillingham knew that he was Frank Burdick—and Dillingham didn't care.

He puzzled over that as the afternoon wore along, getting no farther than he had done with the puzzles of the previous evening. Meanwhile Dillingham and the girl were having themselves quite a time. She was talking about the Big Hole country in terms which let Burdick know that she must have been living here for some little time. He couldn't quite understand her position but guessed that she would be related to some new settler, apparently a person of some substance.

He dozed again, opening his eyes to realize that they were within about five miles of Osage. Already they were on the long downgrade which led out of the last big canyon to the flatlands which had become the region's best graz-

ing area. He heard the brakes squeal again as Slats prepared to make the sharp turn around Calamity Rock, and
then suddenly other sounds broke in. Iron-shod hoofs
rang on the stony trail, and a horseman swung in beside
the coach, a hairy hand shoving a gun almost into Burdick's face. At the same instant a more distant voice yelled,
"Pull 'em up, Slats! This is a holdup!"

Other orders were barked at the driver, but Burdick's
attention was concentrated on the man who was covering
the four inside passengers. The bandit had bent over a
little in the saddle, peering in at the quartet as he rasped,
"No fast moves in there, folks. Yuh heard what the boss
jest said. Keep yuhr paws where I kin see 'em." His face
was covered by a handkerchief but Burdick judged that he
was a young man, red-haired and with a generous sprin-
kling of freckles on his broad nose.

There was a smothered exclamation of dismay from
Miss Lowry but Dillingham was not one to find himself
at a loss for words. "Seems like all the bandits ain't in the
fair city of Butte," he commented. "Must be the James
boys have taken sides in the Clark-Daly feud."

"Cut out the gab!" the outlaw snapped.

By that time other horsemen were in sight, one man
holding a gun on the passengers from the opposite window while a pair of them shouted instructions to the cursing Slats. Burdick realized that they had planned well,
making their play at the one spot in the trail where the
stage was practically helpless. At the bend around Calamity Rock the coach had to come pretty close to a dead
stop, and the outlaws had taken full advantage of the situation. Obviously they were no strangers to the basin.

One of the bandits dismounted and began to haul something out of the boot while the freckled man seemed to
take his cue from a leader and growled a new order at
the passengers he was threatening. "All right, now, you
folks. Climb outa there! Hustle it up, too!"

There was an instant of hesitation, but Miss Lowry
broke in quickly. "We'd better obey orders. Some of these

gunmen are quite hasty with their trigger fingers." She seemed calm enough, merely passing on a piece of sound advice.

The outlaw chuckled loudly. "Plumb good figgerin', sister. Come on outa there, all of yuh." He waved the gun particularly at Burdick. "Twist the tail o' that door handle and let 'em out!"

Burdick shoved the door open and started to move, only to collide with Dillingham who had slid sideways at the same instant. The two men grinned wryly at each other, and Burdick pulled back a little. "You first, Doctor," he said, the mockery in his voice partly a matter of annoyance at the whole situation.

Dillingham grimaced but seemed content to let a whimsical humor cover his own anger and uneasiness. "Thank you, sir," he said with solemn politeness as he stepped out into the open.

Burdick started to follow but the door was jammed back against him, almost crushing the foot he had extended. He pulled away, conscious more of the pain than of the gun which was being waved through the door of the coach once more. Through the fog of pain he knew that the outlaw guard was ordering the remaining passengers to stay in their seats but it was a matter of a minute or two before he could quite realize what the change of orders meant.

There was an exchange of shouts, followed by a querulous protest in the voice of C. C. Dillingham, then a heavy order booming above the rest of the noise. "Get goin', boys! You, too, Slats! And don't bother to look back."

The crack of leather against horseflesh accented the command, and the coach jerked into action, rounding the sharp angle of the trail at a pace which threatened disaster. Two of the outlaws continued to lash the horses until the stagecoach was bowling along madly, then they dropped back, a couple of shots serving to remind Slats of the orders they had given him.

Burdick suddenly remembered the gun which was still

in his belt. Pulling it hurriedly he stuck his head out of the window but quickly changed his mind about firing. It would be a matter of wild shooting now and he might only draw fire. With the girl in the coach he had to avoid that.

Still, the move had given him a quick glimpse of the scene behind them. There were four mounted outlaws, two of them apparently most concerned with the business of getting Dillingham into the saddle of a spare horse. One of the others was watching the retreating stage while the fourth man was already riding away into a gully which branched out behind Calamity Rock. It was the last man who caught Burdick's attention. The fellow was balancing an awkward burden across his saddle horn, a burden consisting of a tin trunk bearing the neatly lettered *Frank L. Burdick, M.D.*

"My trunk!" Burdick heard himself grunt. Then he was hanging on for dear life as the stage rattled over the stony trail, the driver fighting to regain control of his team.

They reached open country quickly, and Slats halted his team, calling down to the inside passengers as soon as the vehicle was stopped. "Anybody hurt down there?"

Burdick glanced at the colorless lips of the girl and saw that she was trying to work up a reassuring smile. "We're all right," he called back. "The shots must have been fired in the air, I think."

Both the driver and the box passenger jumped down then, and Burdick opened the door so that they might hold a brief conference. "What were those men trying to do?" he asked. "And why did they kidnap Dillingham?"

"That was the feller's name, was it?" Slats commented. "Know anything about him?"

"Very little. He was selling patent medicine—I should say *fake* medicine—on the streets of Butte last evening."

Slats scratched his head with long, grimy fingers. "Mebbe some o' the gang needed a tonic," he suggested with an air of elaborate humor. "Plumb queer sort of a holdup, if yuh ask me. They busted outa that niche like a gang of old-time bandits but all they steal is a medicine show faker and his trunk."

"It was *my* trunk," Burdick corrected. "If they were trying to get a doctor and his instruments they certainly made a grave mistake."

"They sure didn't make none on the rest o' the setup," Slats growled. "Ketchin' us there at the rock makes it look like they knowed the country."

"And they knowed yo', too," observed the miner who had been riding inside. "Seems like I heard one of 'em hail yo' by name."

Slats didn't seem to like that. He jerked a thumb toward the coach and started for his box. "We better git goin'," he decided hastily. "Only a half hour to Osage so we'll let Sheriff Hickey take over. Sooner he gits the information the better."

The bearded man grinned but said nothing until the stage was once more trundling along the valley road. Then he asked Burdick, "Got any idee what they wanted o' yore trunk, mister?"

Burdick had a lot of ideas, most of them leading to no apparent conclusion. He elected to keep the important ones to himself, evading rather neatly. "Perhaps I could guess," he said quietly. "I'm a physician and that trunk contained a small quantity of medical supplies as well as some surgical instruments. This man Dillingham has been playing the part of a quack doctor and it's just possible that he has ideas about branching out a little. This could have been arranged between him and the outlaws so as to get him into possession of materials he could not have bought legitimately."

"It sounds pretty farfetched to me," Miss Lowry stated, her glance keen on Burdick as she spoke. He couldn't tell whether she was honestly doubting him or merely defending the man who had made himself so attentive to her during the early part of the trip.

Burdick didn't argue. "I offered it only as a wild guess," he reminded her. "There may be an entirely different explanation."

"It'll shore have to be a queer one," the miner growled. "That was as crazy a holdup as ever I seen. One trunk and a gabby passenger! What kind o' loot is that?"

That seemed to sum it up pretty well. At least the conversation didn't progress much beyond that point in the remaining minutes before they rolled into Osage. Burdick had a hunch that the girl wanted to say more but was purposely holding back. Which was all right with him; he wasn't in any mood to discuss the suspicions which were strong in his own mind.

Sight of Osage once more made him aware of the changes which could be wrought by a lapse of five years. Many of the old familiar buildings were unaltered but there were numerous new ones, enough to make the town considerably bigger than the Osage he had known so well. The old frame bank building stood across the single street from the stage station just as Uncle Jeff had arranged it when he took over the stage line. Proctor's store still seemed on the point of falling into the street. So did the Beaver Head Saloon. The rickety old calaboose, Kennicott's Hotel, Doc Dolan's forlorn little house, and Bob Davies's gun shop were all much the same. There was a nostalgia in that much of the scene, but Burdick was a stranger to the rest of it. The big, newly painted house up the hill, the cluster of frame buildings beyond the hotel, the new stores—all contributed to an Osage he did not know, an Osage which must have picked up some of the growing pains of Butte and the other mining camps.

Somehow the sight brought an unreasoning resentment. Vaguely he blamed the town's growth for Uncle Jeff's murder. He would have liked to remember Osage as part of a dimly pleasant past. Instead he realized that it was the symbol of a troubled present, a present which included murderous attacks and banditry.

The stage pulled around into the lane beside the stage station, preparing to discharge passengers before moving on to the stables at the rear. The old days of hard-driving

stage lines with their relay stations were over in this part
of the Rockies. The railroads were handling everything
but local travel so layovers were expected. Anyone going
beyond Osage would have to wait until the morrow.

A man came out of the station doorway as Burdick
stepped out of the far side of the coach. He was heavy-
bodied, red-faced and just a little bald on top. Burdick
recognized him as Virgil Stroud, the man who had acted
as Uncle Jeff's helper and partner since the stage line first
went into operation. Here was one part of the picture
which had not changed, not that it was particularly grati-
fying. Stroud had never been a prime favorite of young
Frank Burdick—and vice versa.

"Had a holdup, Virgil," Slats announced loudly.
"Dangedest holdup I ever seen in all my borned days. All
the bandits done was to steal a trunk and kidnap a feller.
Never bothered nothin' else."

By that time a hostler had come out to take the heads
of the lead horses so the driver promptly dropped to earth,
adding details to his hasty summary of the story. Burdick
could see the expression of alarm that came over the
agent's red face, an expression compounded of several
emotions. Stroud was angry, alarmed, just as any agent
would have been at finding his company involved with
bandits. But that was not all of it. The man's fright was
too great, too personal.

Suddenly Stroud looked past Slats's shoulder and met
Burdick's eyes. Instantly most of the red drained out of
the pudgy features. He swallowed hard, then scowled de-
terminedly. "Frank Burdick, hey?" he growled. "About
time ye showed yer face! Not that it's doin' much good, I
reckon, judgin' by the way ye seem to bring bandits with
ye!"

Burdick ignored the ill nature of the attack. He would
have expected something like it from Virgil Stroud, anyway, and now he had a hunch that it covered something.
"What do you mean it's about time?" he demanded.

"I mean it's about the time a man might have expected

ye to show up. Yer uncle has been writin' for ye this whole
year but ye wait 'til he dies and there's a legacy to grab."

This time it was hard to keep back the retort, particularly since Burdick realized that Miss Lowry had stepped
down from the coach and was listening to the angry indictment. He held his anger, however, merely staring Stroud
down before asking, "Where's Tex Hickey likely to be at
this time of day? That trunk was my property and I want
the law to get after it as soon as possible."

"Likely in his office," Stroud retorted sourly. "That's
where he usually loafs."

Burdick turned on his heel and started diagonally across
the street, too angry to even trust himself with a farewell
word to the girl he realized was looking after him with
an air of perplexed curiosity.

Chapter Four

TEX HICKEY WAS A BIG BEAR of a man, broad as Virgil
Stroud and even taller than Doctor Burdick. Sleepy eyes
always seemed to peer perplexedly from behind a mass of
black, curly whiskers but Hickey was not as stupid as he
looked. His laziness had a way of exploding into abrupt
action, as sundry evildoers in the Big Hole country had
found out to their dismay.

Tonight, however, there was no sleepiness in the look
he gave Frank Burdick. There was surprise, a show of irritation—and none of the usual Hickey humor.

"Dang near time yuh got here, Frank," he growled.
"Not that it's soon enough." He did not offer to shake
hands although he had been a good friend to young Frank
Burdick in the old days.

"That's just what Stroud said," Burdick told him, turning away for a moment while he found a chair across from
the lawman's spur-scarred desk. It gave him a chance to
shake off the quick resentment at his reception and also to
frame the statement he wanted to make.

"A lot of folks will say it," Hickey told him dourly.

"Then here's my answer. I have not had a letter from my uncle in nearly a year. I didn't know he was dead until I saw it in a newspaper in Butte last night."

"What?" There was disbelief as well as astonishment in the word.

"But let it go for now. Time later to thresh that out. Just at present I'm here to report a holdup of today's westbound stage. It happened at the sharp bend around Calamity Rock. The bandits kidnaped a man named Dillingham and stole a trunk containing my professional instruments and medicines. I think they were headed up into the Flatheads, probably by way of Reveille Canyon."

Hickey sat up worriedly. "A holdup, hey! Gosh, I thought the old days of stage bandits was done. What else did they steal?"

"Nothing, I believe. I'm asking you to ride out there while the light holds. Get a line on which way they started so you can trail them tomorrow." He knew that he sounded a little stiff but he was having a hard time trying to swallow his anger at the way he had been greeted. The people of Osage had already condemned him, he realized, blaming him for his apparent neglect of Uncle Jeff. For a moment he wanted to tell Hickey his story, depending on old-time friendship to help out. Then he realized that there might be a connection between this attitude and the attack which had been made upon him in Butte. The man—or men—who had tried to keep him from reaching Osage probably would be the same as the ones who had promoted this community resentment against him.

Accordingly he shut his lips a little grimly and turned away, not even waiting for Hickey's grumbling compliance. It wasn't pleasant to have everyone as either an enemy or a critic but the time was not yet ripe for confidences. As yet he couldn't tell which persons were to be trusted and which were to be suspected.

Hesitating only briefly while he considered his next move he went into Proctor's general store to purchase extra underwear, socks, and shirts as replacements for what had been lost in the stolen trunk. Abe Proctor was a taciturn sort, his grunted salute no more than would have been given to any other customer. His words didn't even hint that he knew Frank Burdick had been away but there was a brusqueness in his manner which was too sullen even for Abe. Evidently the anti-Burdick feeling was widespread in Osage.

Carrying his bundle under his arm Doctor Burdick walked on down the street to Kennicott's hotel, meeting no one he knew. The Valley House, Samuel Kennicott, Proprietor, was rather pretentious for a town of the size of Osage. Partly that was because the pose had been profitable and partly it was a matter of Sam Kennicott's preference. Ever since Sam had gotten into politics he had been a pompous sort of individual and his hotel reflected its owner's personality. There was even a second story on one part of the building and the bar had been pushed around to the side instead of fronting on the street as was the custom with most saloons. It was an arrangement which permitted the Valley House to hold itself out as a suitable stopping-place for such lady travelers as happened to stop overnight in Osage.

Coming out of the twilight into the darkened front room which served as parlor and lobby, Burdick didn't even see that there was anyone in the place until he had taken several strides toward the lighted doorway which led to the bar. Then a woman's voice asked calmly, "Did you report the holdup, Doctor Burdick?"

He swung abruptly to face the girl who had been on the stagecoach. She had been standing beside one of the curtained front windows so he realized that she must have seen him while he was still on the street.

"I reported," he told her. "When did you learn my name?"

"At the stage station a few minutes ago. Not that I didn't suspect before. I happened to get a glimpse of the name painted on the trunk which the outlaws carried away—and you said it was your trunk."

He laughed shortly. "Easy as that, was it?"

"Don't discount my ability," she protested. "I thought I was being pretty smart." Then her voice dropped a little as she added, "Also I think I understand something else. I think I know why Mr. Dillingham was kidnaped."

Before Burdick could reply a shadow blotted out the light from the adjoining room and Sam Kennicott came in. Sam had put on a few extra—and unnecessary—pounds since Burdick's departure from Osage but otherwise he looked pretty much the same. He still affected an immaculate white shirt, a never buttoned fancy vest, overly tight pantaloons, and congress gaiters. That was his indoor costume. On the street his attire always suggested a prosperous gravedigger, a fact which he cultivated purposely, feeling that it gave his political aspirations a certain dignity.

"Sounded like Frank Burdick in here," he boomed, the big voice coming from deep inside the massive figure. "I heard yo' was back, Frank. Welcome home." He took Burdick's hand in a fat fist, talking volubly while he pumped at it. Even allowing for Kennicott's carefully cultivated political manners it was pleasant to be greeted so cordially.

"Glad to find someone willing to shake hands with me," Burdick told him, finding an opportunity to get in a word. "So far everybody has acted as though they suspected me of carrying the hoof-and-mouth disease."

"Been talk," Kennicott told him soberly. "Folks think yo' didn't act right decent toward yore uncle. I'm mighty certain yo' musta been busy finishin' up yore doctorin'. Told 'em so—but they still didn't stop cussin' yo'."

"I was busy," Burdick told him tersely. "But not that busy. I'd have been out here if I'd known Uncle Jeff wanted me. The fact of the matter is that I haven't heard from him for nearly a year. In that time I must have written him twenty letters—without a single reply."

"Yo' don't say! That's mighty odd. Yore uncle told me only about three-four weeks ago that he'd been writin' to yo' fer six months without gettin' a mite of an answer."

"Probably he did," Burdick retorted. "I'm just beginning to realize that there has been a heap of crooked work going on around here. Interfering with mail was only a small part of it. Sam, have you got a good room for me for a few days?"

"Next best one in the house," the landlord boomed. "Miss Lowry got first pick." He guffawed genially. "I reckon yo' two met, hey? Seems like yo' musta been among them present at the recent bit o' outlaw excitement."

"We were there," Burdick retorted. "It was my trunk that was stolen. That's why I'm now descending upon your establishment with a bundle."

"Yore credit's good," Kennicott assured him, lighting a lamp and moving around behind a shiny new desk. The furniture in the place generally seemed new but the register was the same old ledger book which had been in use as long as Burdick could remember.

There was an instant while Kennicott fumbled with the book, an instant seized by Miss Lowry to murmur, "I'll talk to you later." Then she was headed up the bare flight of stairs which led to the upper floor.

Kennicott winked elaborately, a gesture which contorted the whole broad face. "Seems like yo've got off to a good start with Jane Lowry, Frank. Not bad, son, but look out for Rusty Aiken. They claims as how he's fixin' to match up with Jane."

"Rusty Aiken?" Burdick repeated, not bothering to deny the fat man's quick assumption of a budding romance. "Who's he?"

"Ramrod for Lowry. I reckon he came into the basin about the time yo' headed East. Lowry supplies the dinero and Aiken bosses the job."

"What job?"

"Didn't yo' know? It was Lowry that bought out Diamon K."

"Probably I heard the name but I didn't remember. Uncle Jeff handled the deal and I didn't interfere."

"Mebbe yo' should. Jeff got a good price, but Lowry and Aiken have shore run Montana bunch grass into a nice pile of money."

"More power to them," Burdick replied. "We sold out because Uncle Jeff had other interests and I was set on studying medicine. Naturally I'm not complaining because the buyers picked up a bargain."

Before Kennicott could reply there was an interruption in the form of a dumpy little man in a round hat and shirt sleeves. He bustled in briskly, talking almost before he was fairly through the doorway. "Hi there, Frank Burdick! I just heard about you bein' in town. What's the story on the robbery and where have you been all the time?"

There was more to it than that but his continuing string of queries suffered a break when both Kennicott and Burdick interrupted. Question-Mark Turpin had been editor and publisher of the Osage *War Cry* ever since that small but somewhat rowdy paper first came into existence. He was more of a showman than a journalist, a fact which kept the paper interesting even though it kept Turpin in a constant wrangle with people he misquoted or libeled. He was short, squatty, round-faced, and generally disheveled, haircuts and shaves being matters for odd moments when his mind was not occupied with anything else—which was seldom.

Burdick accepted the pudgy, inkstained hand, murmuring a polite greeting before turning his head to ask Kennicott, "Got a place where we can talk a bit, Sam? I suppose I've got to make some kind of a statement for old nosy here, so I might as well get my story told for both of you at the same time."

It was clear that the hotel man wanted nothing more. He turned promptly and led the way back through a short hallway into a room which evidently was his own private sanctum. "We're alone," he said briefly. "Fire away."

Burdick grinned. Kennicott made it sound as though this were to be a secret session. With Question-Mark Turpin on hand that was a bit ridiculous. "I'm not trying to hide anything. Rather the opposite. Since I struck town I've been given to understand that folks don't think too highly of me because I didn't come sooner. It has been inferred that I refused to heed my uncle's call. Actually I have not had a letter from my uncle in nearly a year. During that interval I wrote him a number of letters—and now I'm led to believe that he wrote to me rather frequently. Yet I received no mail from him and he received none from me. The conclusion seems obvious. During the past year someone has been systematically intercepting my uncle's mail."

"Did you get notice of your uncle's death?" Turpin asked, scribbling notes even as he talked.

"I did not. My first information about it came from a crumpled paper in Butte last evening."

"Now that's dam' funny," the newspaperman said. "I happen to know that Tex Hickey wired you about it."

"Wired? I didn't know there was a telegraph line here."

"It wasn't a direct wire. Hickey sent the message by one o' the stage drivers. He was to send the wire from Butte."

"Which driver?"

"Slats McGill, I think."

"When was it sent?"

Turpin ran inkstains into his hair as the pudgy fingers clawed thoughtfully. "Let's see. Your uncle was killed on the tenth. There wasn't any eastbound stage next day so the message didn't leave here until the morning of the twelfth. It should have been sent from Butte that night or the next day."

Burdick nodded. "I believe the item in the Butte paper was published on the fourteenth. I was in Chicago—at my regular address—until the evening of the twenty-fifth. I never received any such wire."

"Gosh, Frank," Kennicott rumbled. "I've been blaming you for not comin' home. This looks like somebody's trying to get away with somethin' kinda sneaky."

"No doubt about it in my mind. I just want to know

why."

Turpin was studying him from beneath half-closed lids. "Then you didn't know your uncle was sick, is that it?"

"Sick? No. How sick?"

"He wrote you, telling you about it. That much I'm sure."

"I never received such a letter. How sick was he?"

Turpin shrugged. "I don't think he knew. Sometimes I didn't think Doc Dolan knew. Maybe that was why your uncle wrote you. Dolan kept sayin' it was some kind of fancy indigestion, but your uncle kept getting more and more peaked. That's when he wrote this letter I mentioned. He kinda thought you'd be full of the latest scientific ideas and maybe could spot something Dolan had missed."

Burdick stared from one solemn face to the other. "Is that fact generally known in Osage?"

Kennicott's laugh was a mirthless rumble. "Turpin knew it. Ain't that answer enough?"

The newspaperman stammered a defense, but Burdick waved it aside. "I'm not blaming you, Question-Mark. I'm just trying to see the picture. Folks in Osage figure that I turned down the pleas of a sick man. No wonder they haven't been overly cordial to me."

"I'll try to explain it for you," Turpin proposed.

"Don't. I can stand ill-feeling for a time. Maybe it'll help to smoke out some truth about more important items. Anyway, I'm not in a position to prove a thing I say so I'll not be put in a position of begging folks to believe my story."

"Don't be so damned proud." Turpin grimaced, his manner of saying it taking all trace of sting from the words. "Let me tell folks why you stayed East."

"Nothing to tell. I was worried about not hearing from Uncle Jeff but the last few months of my work were pretty important. I decided I'd finish the course before I came out to see why he'd turned silent. That's nothing to write up in a newspaper and I'd rather you didn't get started on the business of the intercepted mail. People wouldn't believe it anyway, and if we keep quiet we may have a better chance of finding the responsible party."

"That part hadn't oughta be hard," Kennicott told him. "There's folks in this town stood to gain by Jeff Burdick's death. They likewise figure to keep Jeff Burdick's nephew outa their hair as long as they can."

Burdick wheeled to face him directly. "Name them, Sam!" he snapped.

"I don't know fer sure. All I got was a hint about what was in yore uncle's will. Mark Clay has it. He's executor, I hear. He read it to Ellen Davies, Stroud, and Dan White-side. All three of 'em stand to gain somethin' by his death."

Burdick had to think hard. Mark Clay was a local attorney of considerable skill but dubious reputation. Whiteside had been Uncle Jeff's partner in the local bank just as Virgil Stroud had shared the express and freight business. "Who's Ellen Davies?" he asked.

"Yo' remember Bob Davies, the gunsmith, don't yo'?"

"Oh. You mean his daughter? The tubby kid with the pug nose?"

"That's the gal—only she's some growed up now. Three-four years ago she started studyin' bookkeepin' and stuff. Fust thing we know she was practically running yore uncle's affairs. By that time he had a hand in half the basin's business so he needed help, perticklerly when he got sick. Ellen was practically an extra right hand for him. Toward the end she was nurse as well as business agent for him. Understand," he added hastily, "I'm not accusin' Ellen. I'm not accusin' anybody, for that matter. I'm just telling' yo' who had a place in Jeff Burdick's will."

"I understand. Were there any others?"

"I don't know fer sure. I'm talkin' rumors, yo' know. There was others in the basin with dealin's, of course. Yore uncle and me once bought up some dead mine claims so I reckon yo' kin even add me to the list." His wry grimace hinted that he didn't remember the transaction with any great pleasure.

Turpin was beaming importantly now. "Sounds like it's my turn to speak my piece," he cut in. "Sam musta missed one point in the will—or maybe his gossip source wasn't the same as mine. Anyway, it seems your uncle got so sore about your not coming home that he changed his will about three weeks before he was shot. I don't know the details but it seems that you're to inherit everything he had if you arrived by a certain date. Otherwise the property was to be divided among the others."

"What do you mean, a certain date?"

Turpin shrugged. "I'm not able to quote exactly, remember. As I got it your uncle had been told that he could only live a month or so. Dolan told him, I think. So he started making his plans, calm as could be. He even estimated the date of his probable death, allowing a couple of weeks for his own toughness to fool Dolan. If you didn't show up by that date you lost out."

Burdick stared. "You probably won't believe me when I tell you that I'm not much excited about the inheritance. My father left me his share of the valley property, and I'm prepared to practice medicine on my own. Still, I'd like to know what date was mentioned in that will. It might answer a few questions."

"That's easy," Turpin told him, grinning. "The deadline is tomorrow. Want to know anything else?"

"Sure I do." Burdick did not respond to the grin. There was only a grim anger in his voice as he said, "I want to know who killed Uncle Jeff. I want to know who interfered with the mail. I want to know who tried to kill me in Butte last night. I want to know who staged that crazy holdup this afternoon. There are a lot of other questions I expect to work on but those are the first ones I propose to hammer."

"Gosh!" Sam Kennicott rumbled. "Do yo' figure it was all the same feller?"

"Likely. Right now I'm guessing it was."

"Could be."

Burdick turned to face the stout man. "Sam, what's the

law situation in Osage now? Is there a town marshal or do you depend on the sheriff?"

"It's all Hickey. I'm still mayor but we ain't got much town organization. Never seemed to need any."

"Got any idea why Hickey didn't find any trace of my uncle's murderer?"

Kennicott shrugged. "No clues."

"But what happened? I've heard nothing in the way of detail, you know."

Kennicott glanced at the newspaperman, and Turpin took the cue. "It happened right after supper one night. Your uncle had been mighty poorly that day and had been home in bed most of the time. Ellen Davies had been with him all day, at the usual chores. She got him some supper about dusk, then went home. It must have been about a half hour later that Tex Hickey heard a gunshot and went over to investigate. He says he was afraid your uncle had committed suicide."

"Was Uncle Jeff that bad?"

"I'm afraid he was. He was in pain most of the time, drinkin' mighty hard to dull the aches. Anyway, Tex found him down in his front room office with a hole in the side of his head."

"But it wasn't suicide?"

"No. There wasn't a gun anywhere in the room and there were no powder burns on him. An open window about five-six feet from him made it seem pretty clear that someone had poked a gun in and killed him in cold blood."

"No tracks?"

"Ground was too hard to show a thing. I know Tex looked hard enough. I was there by that time and helped him. Since then he's been working along the line we've just discussed but he can't get any kind of a lead. Several different people might have wanted to get rid of Jeff Burdick but Tex can't prove that any of 'em did it. For that matter he can't prove that any of 'em didn't. The best suspects haven't got any alibis for that evening."

Burdick was silent for a long minute. Then he spoke briskly, showing none of the depression which had seized upon him. "Thanks for the information, gents. Now, Sam, if you'll point out this second-best room I'm to have I'd like to wash my face and grab a bite to eat. After that I think I'll go calling."

Turpin's eyes narrowed. "Calling, eh? On Mark Clay or Ellen Davies?"

"Neither. I've got some questions to ask of Doc Dolan before I try to talk business with folks like that."

Chapter Five

A SENSE OF PHYSICAL WELL-BEING was helping Burdick to shake off the gloom when he left the hotel after supper. Sam Kennicott's food had always been his biggest political asset, the hotel's reputation extending to its proprietor. Tonight Burdick felt a stronger connection between man and hostelry. The meeting with Kennicott and Turpin, along with the excellent meal, had helped. His spirits had risen a notch or two, enough so that he could ignore the hostile glances of the people he met along the fitfully lighted street. Anyway, it was not so painful to meet that hostility now. Knowing its meaning he was almost grateful for it. These folks were displaying a loyalty to the memory of Jeff Burdick.

He spoke to no one as he strode along, a tall, dignified figure in the well-tailored gray suit and dark Stetson. Once he had dreamed of making such an appearance on the streets of Osage but tonight he was not thinking about himself. Pride of accomplishment and profession had been pushed aside for grimmer interests.

There was a light at a back window of Doc Dolan's shabby little house, but Burdick went to the front door. Somehow he wanted this call to be that of one professional man on another, not a casual visit such as young Frank Burdick might have made on an older friend. He went in without knocking, passing through the darkened waiting-room and heading straight for the part of the house where Dolan had his living-quarters. There was the usual odor of drugs in the air but somewhat more clearly came the well-remembered reek of alcohol. Doc was drinking again.

Burdick knew a moment of anger and apprehension but he quickly saw that the old medico had not reached an advanced stage of intoxication. Doc was sitting in an armchair at the kitchen table, his white head down on folded arms in a little cleared place where dirty dishes, old papers, and empty bottles had been shoved aside. After a few more drinks Doc would stagger across to the unmade cot and sprawl there until the periodic spree was over. That had been his habit for so many years that the basin had become accustomed to watching for these debauches, always dreading the chance of a major emergency while the old man was in a stupor.

"Doctor Dolan!" Burdick snapped.

The white head came up slowly, rotating on a thin neck as bleary eyes tried to focus on the intruder. "H'lo, Frank," Dolan said finally. "Got home, hey?"

He reached for a partly emptied quart of brandy, but Burdick beat him to it, putting the liquor out of reach.

"Listen to me, Doctor," he said, still snapping off the words in an effort to catch the dazed man's attention. "I want to know what was wrong with my uncle."

"He—he was shot."

"I know that. I've also been told that he was dying. I want to—"

He broke off as Dolan let his head sag again. Burdick wanted to kick him but instead he crossed to the iron sink with its pitcher pump. A few strokes gave him good cold water in abundance. Filling a bucket he turned back to pour it over Dolan's head, ignoring the protests until the old man was thoroughly soaked. Then he began to rub him energetically with a coarse kitchen towel, talking cheerfully as he did so.

"Remember the first time I did this to you, Doc? I was just a kid but I had to get help for that waddy who had been shot at the Big Hole Saloon. I tried this and it worked. You saved the fellow's life—and I was proud as punch. I felt I'd had a share in it. That was when I made up my mind I was going to be a doctor and save people. Remember how I hung around with you every chance I had after that?"

He went back for another bucket of water, still talking as he ignored the somewhat more rational protests of the older man. This time he had to hold Dolan while he sloshed the water over his head but he did the job with grim thoroughness. More toweling and more reminiscent talk followed until finally Dolan summoned his strength to escape. Then Burdick stood back unsmiling.

"What the hell's the idea?" Dolan sputtered, angry but almost sober.

"Sorry, Doc. I want to know something—and maybe I couldn't wait for you to work your way through this one. What was wrong with Uncle Jeff and why did you tell him he had only a few weeks to live?"

Dolan coughed, shook his head a couple of times, and glared. "I told him that because he hounded me for the truth. The man was dying on his feet."

"Of what?"

"Cancer. That's what!"

"Did you tell him that?"

"No. Folks don't know much about cancer; it mostly scares 'em. I told him he had digestive troubles. Then, finally, he wouldn't be fooled so I told him almost the truth."

"How many other people knew?"

"Most of his friends. He told 'em himself. I guess it wasn't any secret for the last couple of weeks before he was killed."

"Yet somebody killed him. Somebody who couldn't wait for the death which was just around the corner. Got any idea who?"

Dolan's brief show of energy faded. "Go away, Frank. I'm a sick man. Let me alone."

"You're sick, all right," Burdick agreed. "That's why I'll have to give you more treatment."

Dolan made another effort, looking up with sudden understanding as though he had just remembered Burdick's new status. "All right, Frank. You understand." He was almost whining now. "I've got to have a drink. Go read my case book. That'll tell you all you want to know." He reached for the bottle again, and this time Burdick made no move to stop him. When Doc reached this stage he was hopeless.

There was a long drink by the little man, a renewed invitation to read the case book, then another drink. Burdick watched unhappily while Dolan went back to the still-wet chair and slumped into it. There was not much use in trying to teach an old dog new tricks. Better to let Doc get his spree over and out of his system for another month or six weeks.

However, he reached for the battered book which he knew was Dolan's case book. Actually it was a sort of diary, as Burdick well knew. He had studied it many times in the days before going East to start formal medical education. From it he had learned many things, among them that this book was Dolan's way of helping his own memory over the blank spots. Dolan knew his own weakness, and this diary was his attempt to make some professional compensation.

Burdick leafed through it hastily until he located a date just about one year in the past. Then he began to read, skimming some sections and reading others with care. It took five minutes for him to find the record of Jefferson Burdick's first call for help. Dolan had obviously been entirely sober at that time. The notes were clear, the handwriting steady, but the old doctor had been troubled. He had written almost argumentatively of his diagnosis, as though he didn't quite believe it but wanted to convince himself. *Acute Indigestion,* he labeled it then.

Three pages later there were detailed symptoms, including a record of recurring abdominal pains. This was repeated about a week later but this time the handwriting was sprawled, uneven, and partly illegible. Likewise the text was inclined toward garrulity. Doc had been starting on one of his sprees at that point and mentioned cancer in almost maudlin phrasing. *I prefer to keep this knowledge to myself,* he had written. *No man cares to know that his life thread is measured. To an old friend I can not be so brutal. But Jefferson Burdick is dying of cancer.*

There was more in the same vein as the days went on, and Burdick's face clouded as he read the accumulating evidence. Of all the incompetent bungling! Doc Dolan might have been a good man for rough country, especially in his younger days, adept at treating gunshot wounds and broken bones—but he had displayed abysmal ignorance here. Any first-year medical student in a decent school would have known better!

He closed the book with a snap, merely glancing at the record of his uncle's actual death. Forcing himself to a calmness he could not feel he crossed to the table and lifted Dolan's head, not too gently. "Doc!" he snapped. "Look here. Is that book right? Did you get the symptoms correctly?"

Dolan let his head sag in what must have been a nod of agreement. "It was cancer, all right," he mumbled.

"Cancer my foot!" Burdick exploded. "Jefferson Burdick had common old appendicitis, you damned fool! You were letting him die out of plain stupidity. It took the intervention of an assassin's bullet to keep you from being a murderer. Go on and get drunk, you old fool! You're no better sober!"

There was no reply from the man at the table, and Burdick swung to leave. He was a little ashamed at his own outburst. Doc Dolan had been a good friend to him many times over. Once he had admired the man's skill. Tonight it had been a bitter blow to discover Dolan's obvious incapacity. Some of that bitterness had mingled with other worries to cause the outrush of angry words. It was never pleasant to discover that an idol had feet of clay.

He started out through the darkened front room but was interrupted by a familiar voice. "I came in without knocking," Jane Lowry informed him from her position near the front door. "I wanted to talk to you and I saw you come here. You might as well know that I've been watching this extraordinary scene almost from the beginning."

For a moment he had to remain silent, unwilling to speak while his emotions were in such a turmoil. The girl's calm admission had increased his rush of anger and he didn't propose to make any more hasty speeches. Better to save the words and avoid the regrets.

"Do you always snoop around this way?" he asked finally, the words almost polite in their intonation.

"It's scarcely a habit. However, I wanted to speak to you in some place less public than the Valley House. So I slipped in quietly—and the sight of your restorative measures intrigued me into being—a snoop."

"And you heard what I just said to him?"

"I did."

"Then forget it. I was speaking to him as one professional man to another. If you repeat it to anyone I'll deny every word of it, even if I have to call you a liar in public."

She moved into the light, evidently not at all disturbed. "You're a loyal colleague," she observed dryly. "And a hard man to like. But relax; I won't tell people how much you despise Doctor Dolan. Anyway, I didn't come here to argue."

"Very well. I'll strike a light and we'll let you get your thoughts out of your system."

"Leave it dark. We'll be safer from interruption."

"You don't concern yourself with local gossips?"

"Not too much. I do pretty much to suit myself. If folks don't like it they can lump it. Now about this robbery today. Have you considered any real reason for it?"

"Several of them."

"And have you heard the terms of your uncle's will?"

The question caught him by surprise but he maintained the same tone of polite attention. "In a general way. Is there a connection between the will and the holdup?"

"I'm guessing there is. I think someone tried to keep you from arriving in Osage in time to collect your inheritance."

He pretended that the idea was new to him. "But no one interfered with me. I arrived in plenty of time—even if I didn't know about the time limit until after I was here."

"Think back to the moment of the robbery," she went on earnestly. "When we were ordered out of the coach today you collided with Dillingham. You drew back with a sort of mock courtesy, saying, 'You first, Doctor' or something like that. At any rate you used the title. Instantly the outlaws changed their orders and told the rest of us to stay where we were."

"By George! That's the catch I've been trying to pick up. I'd reached the conclusion that this was part of a scheme to keep me away from Osage. It seemed like the logical follow-up to a shooting attempt which I survived in Butte last night but I couldn't understand why they grabbed Dillingham instead of me. You've clinched it!"

"Oh, I'm a smart girl," she told him solemnly. "Not that it took too much brain power to suspect what was afoot when outlaws kidnap a man called 'Doctor' and take nothing else but a trunk bearing a doctor's name. I'll even give you another bright thought from my busy little brain. The kidnapers didn't know you by sight or they would never have made the mistake."

"Pardon me if I'm not so impressed by that one. Even I could figure it out. Try this one on your gray cells. How come they didn't know me by sight when someone had already tried to kill me in Butte, someone I suspect of being a man whom I'd already met?"

"Almost as easy," she retorted. "That first man was not in the party at Calamity Rock. He sent word ahead to confederates, supplying them with a description only. Dillingham happened to fit that description rather well."

He nodded in the semigloom, beginning to be inter-

ested in the guarded humor of the speaker as well as in
her reconstruction of the recent events. "Sounds reasonable, although I can't quite understand why the man in
Butte was willing to do outright murder while the outlaw
gang went to the trouble of making it a kidnap job.
Wouldn't it have been easier for them to shoot their victim along the road?"

"We don't know that Dillingham is still alive," she reminded him. "The fact that they took the trunk hints
that they intended to retard identification of their victim."

He didn't like to think about that first remark. Dillingham had been a good fellow in a lot of ways, no matter
what his occupation might have been. Turning away
abruptly he said, "I'm going to take care of Doc. If you've
got any more bright ideas come along and talk while I
work."

She followed him into the kitchen, watching in silence
while he carried the old man bodily to the cot and covered
him up. Dolan was practically unconscious now, only
mumbling a protest as Burdick put him to bed. Apparently he had taken several swift drinks after his brief interval of lucidity and was rapidly going under.

"I thought you were pretty mad at him," Miss Lowry
observed presently.

"I am. But I still remember him as a friend, just now a
friend who needs help in a time which to him is not un-
like a spell of serious illness. I'd do as much for any
patient."

She smiled a little as though recognizing that his argument was not entirely consistent. However she didn't
argue the point. Apparently her understanding was deep
enough for her to appreciate the conflict of emotion which
was tormenting Burdick.

"Better head for the door," he said. "I'm going to blow
out the light."

"Right. I'll hold it open so you can see your way."

He did not reply, attending to the lamp and then standing for a moment until his eyes grew accustomed to the

darkness. Then he went through the house, heading for the rectangle of lesser gloom which marked the open front door. "Thanks for your trouble," he said as they stood there together for a moment. "You'd better go ahead. No point in inviting talk by having folks see us come out together. They might misunderstand."

"Don't be an idiot! I suppose half of the town already knows that I've been in there with you in the dark—chaperoned only by a drunken man. I don't mind if you don't."

He laughed shortly, bitterly. "It isn't likely that my present reputation in Osage will suffer much. Come along."

They walked in silence toward the street, neither of them noticing the dark figure which was approaching from the direction of the main group of stores. It was only when they almost collided with the stranger that Burdick saw, realizing that the other was also a woman, probably a young one, judging by her figure and brisk step. There was a quick murmur of apologies and then they were past, neither offering a comment until they had gone a full hundred feet.

Then it was Jane Lowry who spoke, some of the easy humor in her voice replaced by a touch of regret. "That was Ellen Davies we just met—in case you didn't know."

"Who? Oh, the girl who has been acting as my uncle's secretary?"

"Give her credit, Doctor." The dry humor was back quickly. "The girl ran the whole business for him in the past six months."

"You don't like her, do you?"

"I don't know her except by reputation. I gather that she doesn't approve of me, chiefly because I take a hand in my father's affairs much as she did in your uncle's."

"That seems like an odd reason."

"Nothing personal. She just doesn't like Diamond K intentions. She was the one who backed the idea of your uncle investing in those nesters along the river. That made us what you might call business enemies." She seemed to think Burdick would understand, so he didn't ask questions. Time enough for that later.

"Looks like Tex is back," he said suddenly. "Light in his place. Mind if I leave you and go have a few well-chosen words with him?"

"Meaning that you don't want me trailing along? I'm as anxious to know what he found as you are."

"You're a very frank young woman," he told her, grinning. "So I'll give you a frank answer. I want to see Tex alone. Anyway he won't have anything important to tell yet."

She sighed elaborately. "Some days a girl doesn't have any luck at all. First I lost the interesting Mr. Dillingham and now you're casting me aside. And with all my bright ideas, too!"

He forced himself to enter into the spirit of her banter. "Now you're making me squirm," he complained. "But I'll tell you what I'll do. Either I'll look you up soon and tell you all the news—or I'll find Dillingham for you."

"That's a promise—so I'll add one other bit of advice. Don't expect Miss Davies to greet you with any cordiality when you meet. The light was at her back, you know. She could see us a lot better than we could see her. She has already formed her opinion of you, no doubt, seeing you emerge from Dolan's place with that Lowry girl!"

"Thanks again," he said. "I'll brace myself." Then he cut away, crossing to the calaboose where yellow lamplight announced that Tex Hickey had returned from his preliminary investigation.

He found Hickey in the office giving instructions to a lean young deputy who lounged on a corner of the desk. Burdick knew the younger man well enough. They had ridden the range together many times but tonight Moon Peckham showed no sign of recognition. He simply met Burdick's glance, his thin features expressionless as he failed to return Burdick's casual greeting. Maybe this was just another expression of the town's prejudice toward the returning prodigal; maybe it was something else. Burdick resolved to keep it in mind.

"Find anything interesting, Sheriff?" he inquired, looking past the scowling deputy.

"No time," Hickey growled. "Trail was clear, all right. They headed back into the canyon country. We found a spot where they'd halted and messed around a bit like they musta been fixin' a pack. Then they went on. We didn't have light enough to trail 'em beyond there."

"Goin' out again in the morning?"

"Sure. Moon's startin' out now to round up a posse. It'll take a few good men to handle a trail back there in the mountains." He seemed almost surly, and Burdick remembered that he had not had the time to explain himself to Hickey. Tex still regarded him as a thankless nephew who had neglected his uncle in time of trouble.

"Got a few minutes to talk, Tex?" he asked. "I'd like to tell you about a couple of things—and I'd like to ask some questions."

"Fire away," Hickey invited, still gruff. Peckham shifted expectantly but still did not change his expression.

Burdick told his story, much as he had told it to Kennicott and Turpin and with frequent references to that earlier conversation. To it he added the idea supplied by Jane Lowry. It made a rather convincing tale now that so many items were being tallied up, and Hickey's bearded face showed a marked change. Even Peckham unbent enough to ask a couple of sharp questions. Burdick knew that he was having to work his way back into the good graces of men who had been his friends but so far he was doing pretty well. In another day or so he ought to be getting some co-operation.

"Got any way to prove all this?" Peckham asked finally.

"No. Just my word—and the way the rest of the story hangs together."

"I'm believin' yuh, Frank," Hickey said quickly. "What do yuh figger is the way to work things out?"

"I don't know. I need information before I start making guesses. About my uncle's death, for example."

Hickey told him the official story at some length, adding

nothing to his knowledge since Turpin had already covered the ground. There was even a discussion of Hickey's suspect list but no new facts came forth. It was becoming increasingly clear that someone in Osage had been playing a deep game, covering his tracks well and looking into the future. The only place in the whole picture where clever, calm planning did not show was the murder of Jefferson Burdick. There the killer had displayed either frantic haste or complete idiocy. Killing a dying man didn't seem like the play of the fellow who had worked out the rest of the scheme.

Finally Burdick rose to depart, noting that the lawmen would be on the trail before daylight in the morning. Peckham started toward the door with him. "Mebbe I'd better go along," he suggested, the stiffness gone from his tone. "That Butte gunman might still be around lookin' fer yuh."

Burdick knew a moment of relief but fought it back as he recalled his doubts of Peckham's real motive. "Don't bother," he replied. "Killing me in Butte might have had a purpose. Now that I'm here I don't think they'll take the risk with nothing to gain. You go ahead and make your arrangements for tomorrow."

"Have it yore way," Peckham retorted. "But don't make no mistakes. This town ain't keen on yuh, remember."

Chapter Six

BURDICK WAS FEELING reasonably happy when he left Sheriff Hickey's office and headed for the Valley House. He didn't have much to cheer about, but the shock of Uncle Jeff's death was wearing off a little and the first bleak despair had resolved itself into a grim determination to find the killer. That was ugly enough but he still felt relaxed for the first time in forty-eight hours.

Analyzing his own emotions, much as he would have diagnosed the miseries of a patient, he decided that the evening's events had done something to relieve the strain which had been growing upon him even before he reached Butte. He had known a sense of uneasiness almost since leaving Chicago but had attributed it to a natural feeling of doubt at being on his own. Then, last night, had come plain, stark dismay at the tragic news about Uncle Jeff. Almost immediately that reaction had been complicated by a knowledge of personal danger. He had lived with that combination of troubling emotions all night and all day, only to find himself unfairly condemned in the eyes of Osage citizens. That had hurt worst of all, probably because he didn't know quite how to fight it. Now friends were beginning to accept him and he felt a little easier. It wasn't much but it helped.

Preoccupied with his own thoughts he paid scant attention to the quartet of rough-looking men who were standing just outside the batwings of the Big Hole Saloon. As he had told Peckham, he didn't expect any further personal attacks now that he had defeated the unknown enemy's purpose by actually reaching Osage. Hence it was an unpleasant surprise when two of the loungers suddenly moved to bar his passage along the rickety sidewalk.

In the light from the doorway he recognized both men without recalling the name of either. The lantern-jawed one had been a Diamond K rider at one time—fired for chronic drunkenness, Burdick seemed to remember. The shorter man with the whiskers had lived around Osage for many years, supporting himself variously as miner, bullwhacker, teamster, and part-time ranch hand. Both were hardcases.

It was the taller, younger man who declared hostilities, thrusting out the undershot jaw until he reminded Burdick of a long, lean bulldog. "Well, if it ain't Doctor Burdick!" he exclaimed, stressing the title with an obvious sneer. "And jest look at them purty duds! Chicago shore can make a damfool dude of a feller, can't it!"

Burdick halted, alert but puzzled. He didn't want trouble and he could not understand why it was being forced upon him. "What's the meaning of this greeting?" he asked, maintaining his calmness with an effort.

"Now ain't we perlite!" The belligerent one smirked. "Listen.to the dude, Ike. Sweet as pie, ain't he? Don't sound like a polecat what sudden took on airs, does he?"

The whiskers bobbed, a rumble of agreement coming forth. "Plumb sickenin', I calls him. Town wasn't good enough fer him after he got hisself rigged out with fancy ideas. Not 'til he hustled back to grab the old man's money, that is."

It was merely a bald statement of what a lot of Osage people evidently had been thinking but now there was a difference. Burdick could forgive the thought in the minds of people who were simply being loyal to the memory of Jefferson Burdick. These hoodlums represented no such sentiment. They were simply using the idea as a convenient means of being offensive. Burdick could not guess why.

He watched them cautiously, noting the way the tall one wore his gun and the way the stocky man kept his right hand hovering near the front of his loose coat. Out of the corner of his eye he also saw that the other pair had stepped back a little, evidently not proposing to take a hand in what was brewing.

"I take it you gentlemen do not approve of me," he said smoothly, his voice so low as to be almost inaudible. "Which makes it mutual. So I'll just move along and relieve us both of each other."

He took a step toward the hitchrack. It was obvious that they intended to dispute his passage so he made a move that would prevent a double attack. For the moment the stocky man blocked the other fellow's line of vision.

"No yuh don't, pilgrim!" the lanky one snarled, wheeling around to block further progress and slide in ahead of his partner. "We wanta see what—"

He was swinging a gnarled fist as he spoke, but Burdick was not letting the words divert him from the danger. He ducked under the blow, coming up with a counterpunch that rocked his assailant back into the stocky man. It gave him the open passage he had demanded but he knew better than to continue down the street. There would be no evading this fight until it was settled once and for all.

He waited while the shorter man got rid of his stumbling ally. Then the bewhiskered one rushed in with head down and fists flailing. Burdick met him with the same sharp defense but quickly found that those whiskers covered a rocky jaw. Three solid hooks didn't seem to bother him at all, and for a good half minute they traded heavy blows in savage earnestness. Burdick knew that he was outboxing his man but knew, also, a sense of uneasiness. The punches were not doing much. Then he threw one from far back, landing his fist squarely between the stocky man's eyes. This time the fellow staggered backward, landing against the saloon wall and slowly collapsing to the sidewalk.

By that time the taller one was coming back and there was a rattle of excited voices as men rushed to watch the fight. Burdick could not guess at the mood of the audience. They might be hostile or not but he had no time to consider the matter; the lantern-jawed fellow was lunging forward, a gun glinting in his right hand.

There was a flash of the metal as he swung the gun as a club, then he was caught in the same grip which had vanquished the burly thug in Butte. Doctor Burdick dodged the blow, trapped the fellow's arm, and whirled to get shoulder leverage. This time he even managed to aim his victim, whirling the lanky one through the air so that he crashed sickeningly into the man who was trying to get up. There was a sort of sobbing grunt from one of them and then stillness, the pair of them lying in an untidy heap in the shadows along the wall.

Burdick stooped to pick up the gun his assailant had dropped, then turned to face the half-dozen men who had come crowding out through the swinging doors.

"Well?" he asked, breathless but quietly menacing.

"Damn well," someone retorted with a chuckle. "Who

the hell brung on that tornado?"

"Ask these men." Burdick waved the gun toward the pair who had witnessed the scene from the beginning.

One of them spoke slowly, carefully. "Ike and Perrine jumped this feller. They made a mistake." As a summary it was practically perfect. Not only did it tell the story but it relieved the tension. Men laughed, the talk breaking out again as they asked for more details.

Burdick studied them long enough to realize that most of them were strangers to him although two seemed vaguely familiar. None, however, seemed disposed to take up the quarrel so he spoke quietly, motioning toward the still-silent pair along the wall. "Better look after your friends," he suggested.

No one stirred. He had hoped to surprise someone into admitting a connection, but the attempt was a failure. Finally an old fellow with a fringe of gray whiskers drawled, "They ain't no pards o' mine, brother, but I'll help haul 'em away if yo'll show me how yo' pulled that trick."

There was a quick laugh, and Burdick dropped the captured gun into his coat pocket. The move seemed to relieve the tension entirely, and two men joined the gray-beard in examining the victims. Two others, almost in unison, invited Burdick to have a drink.

Before he could reply there was an exclamation from the shadows. One of the men turned to call Burdick by name. "Better have a look at this polecat, Doc. I think he's got a busted arm."

Burdick turned, hearing a muttered conversation behind him in which someone explained to the others about his identity. He kneeled in the gloom, finding that the man had been correct. The lanky fellow, indeed, had a nicely fractured left arm. Probably had snapped it in the fall.

Burdick stood erect, looking around him at the waiting audience. "I guess you know who I am. Some of you also probably know that Dolan's on one of his sprees. Which means I'll have to treat my own casualties. Somebody get a short board to secure this arm and we'll take our man inside for treatment."

There was a rush to help, and Burdick found himself issuing orders as though he were back in the hospital with an energetic group of orderlies trying to please him. The man referred to as Ike was carried into the saloon and dumped unceremoniously in a corner. Burdick saw to it that he was disarmed but then he ignored the fellow entirely. Meanwhile the rest of the volunteers were busy with the still-unconscious Perrine. While Burdick protected the broken arm from further injury they placed the man on an operating-table contrived by shoving three tables together. By that time quite a crowd had assembled, and Burdick realized that he was practically on trial. Men were watching him interestedly but with an antagonism which they did not trouble to conceal.

He worked quickly and efficiently, getting almost awed co-operation from the original group of helpers. One of them plied Perrine with whisky when he regained consciousness while the others held him down more earnestly than gently. In his student days Burdick had worked before fellow students and critical instructors but he decided that he had never performed his duties before quite so appreciative an audience. These men were enjoying themselves even if some of them remained openly hostile.

Finally the arm was set, properly splinted, and bandaged. Then Burdick glanced around him, reading the various expressions. Men in the background were dubious, skeptical, but the nearer ones were with him solidly. They had seen him work, both as a fighter and a physician, and they were impressed.

He smiled thinly. "Sorry, men. No fees to collect on this job. I'd hardly have the nerve to send a bill."

The laugh was interrupted by the booming voice of the aproned man behind the bar. "Drinks on the house, boys." Then, to Burdick: "Put on that show every night, Doc, and I'll pay you a good commission."

That did it. Everyone tried to talk at once, most of

them attempting to get close to Burdick as they escorted him in triumph to the bar. He knew a brief regret. Too bad he didn't propose to practice here in Osage; he would have made a fine start in securing public confidence.

It was fully an hour before he managed to break away from the celebrants. By that time the weariness of so much constant effort and worry was beginning to make itself felt and he was fighting sleep. Even the knowledge that he had made a small step in the right direction couldn't alter that fact. He was too tired to think about the new puzzle. His attackers had refused to talk but he had learned that both were Diamond K riders. That meant a new question to be answered but Burdick couldn't let it bother him tonight. Tomorrow would be another day.

A clatter of hoofs awakened him at dawn, and he dragged himself tiredly to the window which overlooked Osage's main street. Six men were riding out on the trail to Butte, all of them well armed. Sheriff Hickey was in the lead, and Burdick recognized two of the deputies. One was Moon Peckham and another was the gray-bearded man who had helped to handle Perrine. Maybe that would be helpful. At least the posse would know the story of last night's fracas.

He was about to crawl back into the cot when he noted signs of activity at the stage station. The two regular coaches were getting ready for their early-morning departure, one heading east to Butte while the other would roll on into the southwest through Big Hole Pass. He saw that the miner who had ridden on the driver's seat with Slats McGill was climbing aboard the westbound stage, probably headed for the mining camps of the Bitter Roots.

He climbed back into bed to do some thinking and promptly went back to sleep. When he awakened again the sun was high but he didn't mind. It would be easier not to run into so many people at breakfast.

To his satisfaction he found only two persons in the comfortable dining-room, one of them Jane Lowry and the other a towering young fellow in flannel shirt, Levi's, and Texas boots. Miss Lowry nodded cheerfully, motioning for him to take a seat across from her.

"Good morning, Doctor Burdick," she greeted. "I want you to meet Rusty Aiken. He's foreman at Diamond K. In case you didn't know it we're still using your old brand for our organization."

Burdick nodded. "Good morning, Miss Lowry. Glad to know you, Aiken. I've already made the acquaintance of some of the Diamond K outfit."

The girl frowned, but Aiken seemed to understand. "So I heard," he commented dryly. "I never had too much time for that pair but I didn't expect them to go hog-wild like that. I'm going to fire 'em both as soon as I catch up with 'em." His accent barely hinted at Texas background. Burdick was more concerned with trying to guess his real thoughts. Was he really sore at the men who had made the night's attack or was he covering up?

Between them they managed to tell the story to Jane Lowry. Aiken did his share of the telling, a fact which permitted Burdick to form several opinions. The man was talking cautiously but he knew the facts. Perhaps it was only suspicions which made Burdick feel that his anger was a little overdone.

"I don't like this, Rusty," the girl said, taking up the conversation after a lull in which Burdick placed his order for one of Kennicott's famous breakfasts. "There's something very nasty in this whole situation and I wouldn't care to have Diamond K mixed up in it."

"No more do I," Aiken assured her. "I'll get to the bottom of it."

They exchanged glances and then the girl spoke suddenly as though determining upon a policy of frankness. "You might as well know the setup, Doctor. There's a land rivalry on in the basin. We'd like to extend our holdings because we believe that the future of the valley is in cattle. Your uncle didn't agree. He backed a number of nesters who are at present battling poverty and starvation in the bottom lands. We believe that was a mistake. We think the country won't stand agriculture. It's good grazing land but no more."

"What about the mineral prospects?" Burdick asked quietly.

Aiken replied to the query. "No good. A lot of prospectors have wasted their time back in the mountains on both sides of the basin but every one of 'em has quit in disgust. Over in the Bitter Roots they're still digging but it's mighty clear that we're never going to run any race with the Butte or Anaconda regions. This is cattle country and nothing else."

Burdick nodded. "I can understand that. But I still don't see why I'm concerned."

Jane Lowry uttered a short laugh. "I guess I'll have to explain. We want to get rid of those nesters as soon as possible. They'll fail anyway, so we're trying to buy them out. As your uncle's heir you hold mortgages on almost every miserable farm within forty miles. We'd like to do business with you."

"You didn't mention that last evening."

She laughed again. "Very well. So I buttered you up a bit. It was still a friendly gesture regardless of business angles. Anyway, I wanted to know what kind of interests were behind those attacks upon you."

"Did you find out?"

"No. Did you?"

"No."

"Then we're no worse off than before. As it stands we're not fooling each other. We want to make a deal—with you. So we don't want anyone else complicating the matter so that you'll have trouble with it. If we can help you to clarify the situation we'll be glad to do it. Fair enough?"

"Fair enough," he echoed, meeting her glance. He had a feeling that she wanted to say more but he couldn't decide what it was. Perhaps she was fearful of arousing the jealousy of Rusty Aiken and so was trying to keep the talk impersonal. He liked that idea; it hinted that she was interested in him—and Jane Lowry was definitely a pretty girl. He hadn't forgotten that fact, even in the interesting process of becoming acquainted with her business cleverness.

Almost as though she had been reading his mind she stood up, her voice almost prim as she said, "I'm ready to go now, Rusty. Best of luck, Doctor. Don't hesitate to call on us if you need help."

At exactly nine o'clock Burdick entered the dusty law offices of Mark Clay. It was not an impressive-looking place, situated above Pressley's Livery Stable, but it had been the scene of some very interesting deals in the early days of the basin. Clay was a smart attorney, learned both in the intricacies of federal land law and in the even trickier details of local mining practices. It was generally believed that he had made several small fortunes through dubious practices in both fields, only to lose his gains in follow-up speculations. Jefferson Burdick had employed Clay because he was a smart man. He had watched him because he didn't trust him.

Clay was standing by a street window when Burdick entered, just finishing some remark he had been making to a slender girl in a print dress. He was short, slender, bald, and immaculately dressed in well-tailored tweeds which hinted at Eastern origin. The dark mustache drooped just enough to have a Western flair but it was neatly trimmed, not quite hiding a tight mouth which never managed a real smile. The Mark Clay grin was always suggestive of the cat with canary feathers on its whiskers. Just now there wasn't even a grin.

"Good morning, Doctor Burdick," the lawyer said formally. "I heard you had arrived in town so I asked Miss Davies to be here this morning. She knows more about your late uncle's affairs than I do so it seemed best that she be on hand for your expected visit."

He motioned toward the girl, and Burdick nodded his recognition of the offhand introduction. Actually, he supposed, no introduction should have been necessary. He had known Ellen Davies well enough, recalling her as a tubby kid in yellow pigtails who had helped around her father's shop while he was busy with the mechanical problems of his gun-repair business. Adolescent chubbiness had dropped away with the slight darkening of her hair so that she was a trim young woman with hair that was somewhere between blond and brown. He saw that her features were good and, surprisingly, he recalled the blue of her eyes. In a way she was quite as pretty as Jane Lowry but there was none of the other girl's humor or sparkle in her attitude. Ellen Davies was not greeting him with any faint sign of warmth, and he wondered briefly whether her frank antagonism was due to nervousness at his arrival in Osage or to some other factor.

"Thanks for anticipating my needs," he said finally. "I'm anxious to know just where I stand. So far I've found nothing but confusion in the entire situation. Confusion and more than a hint of threat."

Clay nodded briskly. "I've heard some talk," he admitted. "I understand you claim to have had your correspondence intercepted lately." The tone was almost that of the trial lawyer opening fire on a hostile witness.

"I have not had mail from my uncle in nearly a year," Burdick told him firmly. "Apparently my letters were being stopped over that same period. The same goes for notice of my uncle's death."

Clay wagged his head. "Systematic tampering with the mail would be a rather difficult process. It seems odd that no single letter ever slipped through."

"So I thought," Burdick retorted, stifling his resentment at the obvious doubt in the lawyer's tone. "The only answer is that the tamperer was someone in a position to handle every letter which went in or out. I can attest that there was no such arrangement on my end of the line."

Miss Davies spoke for the first time. "I might have known you'd try to point the finger at me," she said bitterly. "Anyone who would neglect a man like Jefferson

Burdick when he needed help would be almost certain to lie his way out of the responsibility!"

Burdick stared at her in some surprise. Unless she was an excellent actress her anger was not assumed. Nor was she merely angry for herself; her real resentment was over the neglect of Uncle Jeff.

"I'm pointing no fingers," he told her quietly. "So far I can only theorize. Nor can I prove my claim about the interference. Maybe I'll be able to do more about it when I understand the whole situation better. Which is why I came here, if I remember correctly."

Clay accepted the subtle rebuke without expression. "We'll get right down to business. Would you prefer a reading of the will first?"

"No. I'd prefer a summary of my uncle's situation at the time of his death. What property did he hold and who was involved in business relations with him?"

Even as he asked the questions he realized how Ellen Davies was interpreting them. He was making himself sound like the fortune hunter Osage people had thought him to be, a grabber who was interested in nothing but a tabulation of the loot. Just as certainly she was not resenting him as a rival for a share of Jefferson Burdick's property; she simply despised him as a man who had ignored a dying request for aid but had appeared promptly to claim a legacy.

"Skip the actual figures," he said hastily. "I'm mainly interested in understanding motives for murder."

A flashing glance from those almost steely-blue eyes warned him that the added remark had not altered her low opinion of him. She still hated him, and he knew a real regret that it should be so. Ellen Davies had turned out to be a mighty pretty girl, evidently a smart one as well. Too bad he had to meet her under such unfortunate circumstances. She almost made him feel guilty in spite of his own certainty that he was really a victim.

Clay seemed faintly amused at the exchange of glances between the two but he did not comment, contenting himself with one of those feline grins as he settled himself comfortably in a big chair. "I'll outline the situation as briefly as possible," he proposed. "Details and explanations can follow as you request them."

"Good," Burdick replied. "The background first. Later we'll go into detail and study the will." He hoped he was stressing his own disinterest in the money angle. Somehow he wanted Ellen Davies to understand.

Chapter Seven

LAWYER CLAY NODDED importantly, lighting a long cigar before beginning. "It will be a long story, Doctor. Your uncle had a finger in practically every pie in the basin. Except the cattle business, that is. I suppose you know he had sold out there?"

"Of course. My father was his partner on that deal. I inherited Father's share so naturally I knew about the sale of Diamond K holdings. That was the money I used to put myself through medical school."

"Sure enough. Well, your uncle used his share to start a new bank here in Osage, using the same old building. He became its principal stockholder although several local people had shares. A number of the smaller stockholders sold out to him within the first three years so that he owned just sixty-two per cent of the stock at the time of his death."

"Who else was involved? Heavily, I mean."

"Dan Whiteside had the biggest share. Maybe you remember him as a freighter of supplies who made a nice profit running merchandise down to Bannack and Virginia City in the early days. He owns about a quarter share and has been drawing a salary for his active work in running the bank. Your uncle proposed the arrangement, I believe, preferring to stay clear of personal responsibility for business routine."

"Any indication of trouble between them?"

Clay looked toward Miss Davies but she shook her

head. "No trouble," she said flatly.

"Then there was the express and freight line. Since the Utah Northern connected Butte and Salt Lake the stage line has become a local proposition but it still pays. Moreover the company handles most of the freight into the Big Hole and Bitter Root mining camps. Occasionally they haul out test ore for the smelters at Anaconda or Butte. It adds up to a tidy profit every year. Your uncle originally owned the entire company but last year he made Virgil Stroud a junior partner."

"What share?"

"Stroud held a quarter interest. Jefferson Burdick believed in sharing with employees who assumed responsibility. Stroud held much the same position in the transportation company that Whiteside held in the bank. He handled all details of running the business, drawing a salary as well as sharing in the profits. Your uncle also mentions him in his will, making allowances for his services."

"Sounds reasonable so far. Go on."

"Those two were his major interests. Either personally or through the bank he had loaned money on several other enterprises, his mortgages often representing generosity more than smart business. Foreclosures now possible would permit the estate to assume complete or partial ownership of four homestead grants, two local businesses, and a defunct silver mine near Big Hole Pass. In addition he held claims of one sort or another on several mining properties in the Reveille Canyon region. Some of these were personal, some in partnership with Mayor Kennicott. I believe all involved small advances of money, mostly as favors to claim owners at the time of the last election."

"You mean Uncle Jeff and Kennicott bought votes that way?"

"I didn't say so. Your uncle backed Kennicott in the election. They picked up a few miners' votes by the gesture."

"Same thing. Now what about names? Who are the people involved?"

Clay consulted the papers on his desk, checking each as he called them off. "The four homesteaders are named Bigelow, Fishel, Gauntt, and Poor, the last named describing them all. As an attorney I can think of them only as your uncle's pet charities. The local businessmen who owed him money were Robert Davies and Abram Ford. I think you know both of them."

Burdick glanced at Miss Davies. If she was worried over her father being listed as a debtor she did not betray it by any change of expression. Her voice was completely impersonal as she commented, "Both loans made with good security for expansion of the businesses named."

Clay permitted himself another flickering grin, perhaps at her phrasing, and went on. "That's about the whole story. Offhand, I'd add one thought. Mr. Burdick had perhaps a secondary interest in taking a mortgage on those mining claims. There was always the chance that this country might prove to hold some of the ore that has made the Anaconda and Butte districts so wealthy. With a part ownership he would have been in a position to handle freighting of the ore."

"Any of the claims being worked now?"

"I believe not."

"What is your candid opinion of the minor investments you have listed?"

Clay shrugged. "Not very optimistic, I'm afraid. The local men can pay off in time—unless the present boom collapses. The homesteaders are subject to foreclosure and the Lowry interests would be glad to take them over. The mining claims seem to be dead ducks."

"You agree with that estimate, Miss Davies?" He asked the question just as he had asked the others of Clay, impersonally.

"I do." Her manner hinted that she wanted to say more but was determined to stop there.

Burdick gave her an opportunity to change her mind

but when she remained silent he went back to Clay. "Now the will. Can you boil it down for me as you did on the other part? Later I'll read it for myself."

Clay looked him straight in the eye. "You're trusting me pretty far, aren't you, Frank?" he asked, half humorously. "I seem to remember that you didn't think too highly of me when you were around here some years ago."

Burdick met the gaze. "I didn't," he retorted. "Maybe I still don't. But you're a lawyer. I need one. Maybe I should retain you—and watch you."

Clay scowled, then chuckled. "Not a very complimentary proposition—but I'll take you up on it. We'll talk about it when this session is over. For the present I'm representing the estate so I'm prepared to offer services as that representative. Naturally I'll send a bill for that service."

Burdick nodded. "Naturally," he agreed. "There will be no question over a proper fee. Now about the will? What's it like?"

"First a word of explanation. For a period of several months before his murder your uncle knew that he was dying. He—"

"I've talked to Doc Dolan," Burdick interrupted grimly. "And I've seen his case book."

"Then you understand. You will also understand that your uncle had his doubts about Dolan's treatment. He wanted someone with a more modern medical education to look him over—so he wrote to you, asking you to come home. He never received any reply."

Burdick sighed. "I've told my story. Go on."

"Your uncle was resentful, hurt at your—er, apparent neglect. He wrote several times, hesitating about making an alternative trip to a doctor in Salt Lake City or Portland. Finally he sent for me and drew up a new will. In it he makes a peculiar provision which he explains adequately in the document. It's a strange will but it's legal. I'll guarantee that. He provides that his entire estate shall go to you except for three specific bequests of one thousand each to Ellen Davies, Daniel Whiteside, and Virgil Stroud.

"Then comes the joker. After explaining his reason for the provision he directs that the aforementioned distribution of his estate shall take place only in the event that you shall appear in Osage on or before the twenty-ninth day of June, eighteen hundred and eighty-four."

"Which is today," Burdick commented. "Does he explain in the will why he picked that particular date?"

"In some detail. He didn't want anyone to question the eccentricity of the document so he made it clear and reasonable. Dolan warned him that he could not expect to live longer than the middle of the month. He was more optimistic than that but he fully expected to die. He wanted you to inherit—if you came to see him. If you came only upon word of his death he didn't want you to have anything."

"Nice mess," Burdick commented, his lips tight. "I did not come to see him while he was still alive—yet I didn't come upon word of his death. I'm not exactly sure what my moral rights are."

"Wills are not probated on moral rights," Clay reminded him. "Your uncle made his plans, telling me in detail that he proposed to extend the time limit if he should continue to live beyond the time set. He kept hoping, you see, that you would show up. One way or another you're legally entitled to the estate. We don't need to worry over the oddities of how you happened to turn up at just the right time."

Burdick didn't reply. It was hard to realize that Uncle Jeff had so calmly contemplated a specific date for his own death. It was even harder to think clearly about the fatal events which had been behind that contemplation and the even more tragic shooting which had interrupted it.

Almost through a haze he heard Clay's voice continuing. "The will provided that there should be an entirely different distribution of assets should you fail to appear in

Osage between the will's date and June twenty-ninth. All properties and funds of the Big Hole Transportation Company should become vested in Virgil Stroud. All mining stock owned jointly with Sam Kennicott would become sole property of Kennicott. Fifty per cent of the bank stock owned by Mr. Burdick would go to Whiteside and the other fifty per cent to Miss Davies. Miss Davies also would get all other assets, including the Burdick property here in town, various chattel mortgages, and the mine claims in which Kennicott held no share."

"I see. If I didn't care enough to come out here and see him while he was alive I didn't deserve to share in the estate. I don't blame him for feeling that way."

"But you did arrive," Clay pointed out dryly. "As we've already agreed, you can now claim the bulk of the estate, regardless of the various complications which appear to have entered the picture."

"And that means I'll have to arrange for settlement of the estate. Actually I was very interested in finding a suitable location and establishing myself there in a medical practice. This delays my start considerably."

"Why not start in Osage?"

Burdick shook his head. "In the first place I'd set my mind on a bigger city. Now that I've found how willing Osage was to believe the worst of me I'm content to get away from here as soon as possible." He tried to keep the bitterness out of his voice but there was enough of it left to make Clay look up.

"People in Osage have often thought the worst of me," he pointed out, his grin awry. "Sometimes for good reason—but I'm still here. You might do worse than to settle in a growing community."

"Not with so much background of hard feeling. Now give me a quick estimate of the differences felt by these other prospective heirs. Because of my arrival, I mean. How much did it mean to each of them whether I made it or not?"

Mark Clay looked troubled. He stole a side glance at

Ellen Davies, then murmured, "I don't have any such exact figures."

"Make a guess. You've had the estate in your hands long enough to know how it shapes up. I'm not interested in actual records; I simply want to know who had the biggest motives for killing my uncle and trying to keep me away from Osage."

Clay still hesitated, but Miss Davies answered the question in the same precise, impersonal tone she had adopted previously. "Your arrival deprives Virgil Stroud of thirty or forty thousand dollars worth of property, perhaps even more. Daniel Whiteside loses some thirty thousand. I lose something between fifty and seventy-five thousand." She seemed to be daring him to suspect her as the big winner.

"There's more," Clay cut in. "Kennicott loses the chance to become sole owner of some worthless prospect holes. The nesters along the river get you instead of Miss Davies as a mortgage holder. The same is true of her father and Abe Ford. That may appear as a loss to them. Finally, I lose my position as executor. You become executor of the estate simply by qualifying as principal heir. That's also in the will."

"Let's settle that part right now," Burdick proposed. "As executor I wish to retain you as attorney for the handling of the whole affair. Do you want the job?"

"No. It's going to be a headache. But I'll take it."

"Good. Now tell me about one thing you've barely mentioned. If the Lowrys are trying to buy up those nester mortgages they're interested parties."

"That's right. Like the nesters only in reverse. Lowry tried to buy the mortgages from your uncle and was refused. He will make an attempt to buy them from you. He would have done the same had Miss Davies become the holder."

Burdick turned to face the girl. "Would you have sold?" he asked bluntly.

"No. Will you?"

"I can't tell yet. Too early for me to commit myself. I'm

not anxious to remain involved in the business affairs of the basin but I don't propose to make any steps until I know what I'm doing—and until I know what several other people are trying to do."

A sudden disturbance in the street interrupted the talk, Clay frowning in annoyance as men shouted to each other over the noise of hoofbeats. It was Ellen Davies who crossed to the window to look out.

"Trouble along the river," she said quickly. "Harry Poor just rode in on a lathered horse. He's banging on Doc Dolan's door."

"Dolan's on a jag," Burdick growled. "Maybe I'd better go see if there is anything I can do."

He hurried out without waiting for a reply, taking the dusty steps in threes to emerge on the street just as Sam Kennicott crossed to where a man in overalls was hammering at Doc Dolan's dingy front door. Other men were also converging on the hoeman, excited voices repeating the message he had brought to town. There had been some shooting up the river, apparently in a fight over a fence line, and a nester had been badly wounded.

Burdick came up behind the excited farmer just as the man threw the door open and shoved in. Kennicott turned for just an instant, his eyes questioning as he glanced at Burdick.

The younger man shook his head. "Doc's hopeless," he stated. "I'll do what I can."

By that time the three of them were in the darkened rear room where the small figure of Doc Dolan was huddled under a blanket. A half-empty quart of brandy was on the floor by his side so Burdick knew that the old man had regained consciousness long enough to replenish his supply and continue with his spree.

The hoeman cursed bitterly at the sight, and Burdick took over. "I'm Doctor Burdick," he announced. "Where is the patient and what condition is he in?"

There was suspicion in the farmer's eyes but there was also relief. He was glad to find other shoulders for the responsibility he had been carrying, even though those shoulders were those of a stranger. "Ned Fishel's the man," he said hoarsely, big hands held stiffly at his sides. "He got two forty-five slugs in him, one high up on the left shoulder and the other through the meat of his right leg. He bled kinda bad but we plugged up the holes the best we could."

"Where is he?"

"At his place. Oh, I see what yuh mean. It's about six miles upriver."

Burdick snapped fast orders, first to the hoeman and then to Mayor Kennicott. "Poor, you get back there and have a good fire going. I'll want plenty of hot water so get it boiling. Don't let anybody move the wounded man if you can prevent it. Move, now! Mayor, see if you can get me a good horse in a hurry. While you're doing that you won't see me borrowing Dolan's instruments. The bandits stole mine when they took the trunk so I'll have to borrow from my unconscious friend—it being his job, anyway."

Another figure came into the room as Sam Kennicott hurried out, and Burdick looked up to meet the worried blue eyes of Ellen Davies. All the steel was gone out of them now as she asked abruptly, "Are you going out on the case?"

"Of course. A man needs help and Dolan can't go."

"Can I help?"

"You can if you know anything about Doc's arrangements here. I'll want surgical instruments, bandages, a few drugs. Know where he keeps things nowadays?"

"I do." She pointed to a kitchen cupboard. "Quite a lot of things are in there—and I'm afraid you won't approve of their condition." There was a hint of irony in the comment but almost at once she added, "I didn't like it too well when I had to come over here a couple of times and get emergency medicine for your uncle."

Burdick preferred not to talk about his uncle. It was too easy to recall Dolan's stupidity. He found the cupboard all that the girl had hinted. Rusting, uncleaned instruments were scattered hastily on the shelves, drugs shoved aimlessly out of the way without any attempt at classification. It seemed clear that Doc Dolan had been slipping badly during the past few years. Once he had let common sense and a certain native shrewdness partly atone for his lack of formal education, but apparently the brandy had been getting the better of him. Maybe Jefferson Burdick wasn't the only patient he had blundered on.

Burdick worked in silence, selecting the items he wanted and bundling everything into reasonably clean towels. Then he asked Miss Davies, "Do you know anything about this man Fishel's place? Will there be utensils for sterilizing these instruments? I asked Poor to get hot water ready but I didn't think to inquire about details."

"I'm surprised you thought of it now."

"I'm remembering the country. Not much kitchenware up the river when I was around."

"There will be utensils," she told him. "Fishel was moved to his own cabin, I hear. He wasn't far away from it when Lowry's thugs shot him." The bitter anger in her voice showed through the anxiety. It was becoming clear that Ellen Davies had an interest in the upriver country. Maybe it accounted for a rivalry between her and Jane Lowry, a rivalry which Miss Lowry had admitted jokingly.

Still Burdick did not comment on her reference to the Lowrys. He was already hurrying to the door but she passed him before he could reach it, running down the street at a rate which reminded him of the day when Ellen Davies had been the tomboy of the village. He wondered at her sudden haste but did not comment. Sam Kennicott was saddling a big sorrel horse in the side yard of the county building, and for a moment Burdick thought the mount was to be his own. Then he noted the equally sturdy steeldust tied to a near-by fence and knew that Kennicott was going to keep him company. The stout mayor didn't do much riding but with Sheriff Hickey out of town Sam would probably strain a point and go along to represent the law. That suited Burdick well enough. If there was trouble in the basin, as Ellen Davies's remark hinted, he wanted somebody else to handle that part. A man doing emergency surgery couldn't afford to have his attention divided.

Chapter Eight

THERE WASN'T MUCH SAID between them as they rode hard out of town, following the river trail as it wound through the bunch-grass country which had made the Big Hole Basin such a popular grazing area. Not more than fifteen miles ahead was the old Diamond K ranch house, once home to Frank Burdick and once the only real habitation for many miles southwest of Osage. Now there must be several dwellings between the ranch and the town, buildings thrown up by the squatters or homesteaders who had drifted in on the heels of a booming prosperity rumor.

It was when they passed the first of these hasty frame structures that Kennicott broke the silence, panting a little as he called, "Better not push that bronc too hard, Frank. We can't do six miles in a sprint." Burdick felt that the fat man was expressing his own discomfort more than anything else but it was good advice, so he slowed the pace a little.

Motioning toward the building which they had just passed he asked, "Is that a sample of the farms in this area?"

"Just about. Anyway, it's a sample of the places where nesters insist on tryin' to raise crops. Men like Fishel and Bigelow are switchin' over to blooded cattle. That was how come yore uncle backed 'em with cash. He figured it was throwing money away to try dirt-farmin' in this basin but he had a hunch there was room for more cattlemen. He was willin' to finance a try at mixin' Montana bunch grass with fancy breeds of stock."

"Then the trouble between Lowry and the nesters is not a matter of cow outfit against farmer?"

"Nope. Did somebody tell yo' different?"

"Somebody hinted in that direction." He could recall Jane Lowry's exact words but she had certainly implied—but it didn't matter now.

They went through a gate in a seemingly endless barb-wire fence, Kennicott offering a word of explanation as he held back for Burdick to handle the gate. "This wire's a part o' the trouble. The Lowry outfit is all for open range but a couple of the little fellers have fenced their homestead grants with the idea of bringin' in blooded stock and keepin' that stock by itself. It was yore uncle's money paid for that fence."

Burdick didn't comment. It was becoming increasingly clear that he would have to make some investigations of his own before accepting much of the information which had been tossed his way so promptly upon his arrival in Osage. Folks had a way of trifling with the exact truth when they wanted something pretty badly.

Three horses were tied at the corral of the next nester cabin, a small but snugly built log structure. Kennicott motioned toward it as they spotted it from the top of a low rise. "Smoke arollin'," he commented. "Looks like Harry obeyed orders about the fire and the hot water. Must be extra help on hand, too. Horses at the corral."

"Good," Burdick said shortly. He was gathering tension as he approached the place and was not inclined to talk. There was a real emergency coming up and his hospital experience had not been very extensive in the matter of gunshot wounds. His first case was going to be a tough one, a real test in more ways than one. He was going to be on trial in the minds of these farmers much more than he had been on trial last night. Setting a broken arm had been a minor matter; this job would be a dangerous one, in a way as vital to the doctor as to the patient. A good job now might give him stature with the basin's residents and help him to dig out the facts he needed to know. Failure would only add to the difficulties of the situation.

They found Fishel unconscious and breathing heavily. He had been brought to the house, roughly bandaged, and allowed to lie on the kitchen floor. Burdick kneeled quickly, fearful that the handling might have aggravated the injury. That was often the trouble with well-meaning friends; they did more harm than good.

A quick examination made him feel a little easier, so he did not condemn the bad judgment. Instead he merely checked pulse and respiration, then looked around at the three silent farmers and Kennicott.

"We'll have to risk moving him again, men. Try to slide a blanket under him without twisting his body or letting him move any more than is essential. Then get him on the kitchen table and leave the blanket around him."

Even as he spoke he was beginning to unroll the towel-wrapped instruments he had taken from Dolan's cupboard. Certain items went quickly into a kettle of boiling water that was on the sheet-iron stove. Others were laid aside for future use. It was then that a clatter of hoofs near the corral indicated the arrival of another rider.

No one went to look, however, until the wounded man was safely on the improvised operating-table. Then Burdick's attention was caught by the surprise in Kennicott's voice as the fat man exclaimed, "Ellen! What in tunket are yo' doin' here?"

Burdick whirled, the girl eyeing him steadily as she answered the mayor's question. "I can help. I know a little about surgery and nursing."

Burdick hesitated for only a split second. Something in her tone told him that she was not making an idle boast. "Take over here," he directed crisply. "Get something to fish these instruments out of the hot water with. Be ready with sterile forceps and scalpel when I ask for them. Just pass them on call and you won't have to look at the patient." His quick examination had told him that the wounds were ugly ones, not likely to be a pleasant sight for green assistants.

She took his place by the stove, and he went directly to the wounded man, cutting away the blood-soaked garments so as to expose the nasty-looking hole at the shoulder. The wound seemed to have missed the lung but there would probably be shattered bone as well as a slug to extract. That meant a long, messy job with considerable pain to the patient as well as plenty of strain on volunteer helpers.

"Any of you men know how to handle ether?" he asked, not even looking up as he asked the question.

There was no reply, only a sort of gulp from one of them as Burdick removed the rough pad which had been restraining the flow of blood. He looked around and saw that Kennicott was swallowing hard while the man who had carried the message to Osage was pale beneath his tan. The others were little better. All of them might have nerve aplenty for most emergencies but not one was up to the business of treating a wound such as this one.

"What about it?" he snapped, trying to bring them out of it. "Can't one of you stand ready with a can of ether in case this man starts to regain consciousness? You won't have to look at the operation."

The brief silence was broken by Miss Davies. "I handled ether once. I can do it."

"Fine. There's a can in that other bundle. Get it ready if I call for it. Then stand by the instruments. You men take the other side of the table. Look away if you have to but be ready to hold the patient if I give the word. This isn't going to be pretty or easy so brace yourselves for a long session."

For the next ten minutes there was no sound in the little room except for the heavy breathing of white-faced men and the crisp commands with which Doctor Burdick occasionally broke the tension. Then the man on the table stirred a little and started to moan.

"Ether," Burdick said quietly.

Almost before the word was spoken Ellen Davies had moved into the proper place near the patient's head, handling the ether with a handful of cotton in almost professional style. Burdick watched long enough to be sure that she understood what she was doing, then he nodded approval and went on with his work, probing for bone splinters after retrieving the battered .45 slug.

It was a bloody job all the way and he was soaked with perspiration long before he could call it quits and begin to place a dressing on the wound. Even when the shoulder was properly bandaged there was no opportunity to attend to his own discomforts. Shifting his position he went right to work on the leg, quickly discovering that the bullet there had done much less damage, missing both bone and artery as it entered the thigh. Even better it had emerged from the leg, leaving two clean holes which were no trouble at all after the shoulder operation. Finally he stood back, weary but triumphant.

"Thanks, all of you," he said softly, his glance resting upon Ellen Davies. "That was a fine piece of work, nurse. We're mighty lucky you decided to take over."

Before anyone could find words to reply there was a sort of gasping groan followed by the clatter of someone falling to the floor. Instantly Kennicott's rumbling voice exclaimed, "I'll be damned! Harry's fainted!"

The awe in his tone was almost comic and it served to break the tension. There was a nervous little laugh from both Miss Davies and the other two hoemen. They could see the humor in this weakness on the part of a fellow worker, principally because each one of them had expected to do the same thing.

"Let him alone," Burdick advised. "Shock's a funny thing. He'll be all right." He issued new orders and in a couple of minutes the wounded man was in his bunk, groaning again as consciousness began to return.

"Excellent work with the ether, Miss Davies," Burdick said. "He is coming out of it already. Not many experts can hit on the amount that will keep the patient unconscious for exactly the right length of time."

She gave him a curt nod, turning away to aim a sharp comment at Sam Kennicott. "Your turn now, Mayor," she said. "It's time to get a line on the brutes who did this thing."

Burdick interrupted. "The law will kindly go into session away from the patient. And while you're making plans please arrange for attention to be given the wounded man. I'll see him daily but he'll need good nursing for a long time."

One of the Bigelows spoke up. "My oldest gal kin come over. She's right handy at most things and Ma kin git along without her fer a spell. Dave and me will look after Fishel's chores for him."

The others joined in with plans, and Burdick seized the opportunity to return to the kitchen and clean up the instruments he had used. Miss Davies went with him, saying nothing but working busily at the clean-up job.

"You won't need to help any longer," he told her. "Better prod Sam some more and get his investigation started."

She looked up severely. "Is that sarcasm because of the way I urged him a few minutes ago?"

"Don't be so hasty to take offense. You're interested in this fight out here and I want you to feel free to follow that interest."

"And why shouldn't I be interested?"

"There you go, flaring up again. I'm not criticizing your interest. I'm interested myself. The men who jumped me last night were Diamond K riders, I'm told."

That seemed to surprise her and he went on quickly. "You'd have known that if you hadn't been so anxious to hate me. Somehow it's mighty hard to remember that you're the Ellen Davies I used to know."

"So you remember me. I'm flattered." She didn't sound so.

"Nothing flattering in the memory," he told her dryly. "I can't seem to reconcile the efficient business girl and splendid nurse with the fat little kid whose pigtails always seemed to be too tight."

She whirled toward the door, keeping her back to him as she went out. He managed to add, "Mighty nice change since the old days—even if you don't have very good control of your temper."

He was not certain she had heard him but he felt a little better for having expressed himself.

When Dolan's borrowed instruments were safely packed for transport he went out into the yard where Sam Kennicott was listening to the stories of the three farmers. All three were trying to talk at once but Burdick was able to piece out the tale after hearing a lot of repetitions, guided more by the questions Ellen Davies was asking than by any effort on the part of the mayor. He noted that she continued to refer to the gunmen as Lowry riders although not once did Bigelow or Poor identify them that way.

It appeared that Fishel, a bachelor who lived quite alone, had gone out along the edge of the mountain spur which marked his southwest boundary and had run across three men who had been cutting his wire fence. Coming over a rise to catch them unaware he had ridden forward yelling, only to be met with brisk gunfire. That much he had managed to tell Harry Poor before he passed out from shock and loss of blood.

Poor had heard the shooting from his own land south of Fishel's and had even seen the three hard-riding men who dashed back into the mountains toward Dog Robber Gulch. Fearful of just such trouble he had ridden over along the fence owned jointly by himself and Fishel, discovering the wounded man lying on the ground.

"Left to die, the brutes!" Miss Davies had exclaimed at that point.

Poor had made his neighbor as comfortable as possible, stopping the flow of blood with plugs from Fishel's shirt. Then he had gone for help. While Dave and Charley Bigelow went out to bring the wounded man in, Poor had ridden to Osage for Doc Dolan. The rest was pretty well known to all.

"Did Fishel recognize any of the wire cutters?" Kennicott asked.

Poor shook his head. "He didn't say. The pore feller

fainted dead away while he was gaspin' out his yarn. He didn't git to that point."

"But you saw them," Miss Davies cut in. "Did you know them?"

"Too far away. They was crossing that first ridge this side o' Dog Robber Gulch when I seen 'em. Coulda been anybody."

"Anybody on the Lowry payroll!" she snapped. "No one else in this basin has wanted to cut wire or to shoot men who put the wire up." She had ranged herself beside Dave Bigelow, the younger of the brothers. Dave was a hulking young giant with freckles on a broad face that would have been genial had it not been marked by trouble.

"That's just an opinion, Ellen," he muttered. "We ain't got a speck of proof."

"That's right," Kennicott commented, with some show of relief. "The law can't do much without proof."

"Proof!" she exploded. "Do we have to have the whole valley in a riot before anyone will make a move to stop these killers?"

"Take it easy," Dave Bigelow advised. "We don't know what happened. Ned's gun was fired. Mebbe he shot first."

"What difference does that make? They were cutting his wire—and they left him on the ground to die. I think it's time somebody started getting some action around here!"

Burdick thought so, too, but he kept his voice dull as he started across toward the bronc which Kennicott had borrowed for him. "I think it's time I got back to Osage. I'll be out to see the patient tomorrow. Miss Davies, let me know when I may trouble you for a further interview. I'm quite anxious to get matters settled."

She didn't even reply, and he mounted without looking back, only venturing a brief salute when he was turning the bronc's head toward town. The nesters returned the gesture cordially enough but Miss Davies didn't even look in his direction. And that gave him another question to ponder as he rode the valley trail. Why was Ellen Davies so interested in the land feuds of the basin—especially now that she did not look forward to a mortgage holder's interest in those lands?

He hadn't thought of any good answer when he reached town so he used his time to take care of several routine matters, first returning the pony to the livery stable and the borrowed instruments to the still-befuddled Dolan. After that he picked up Mark Clay and had the attorney take him to the comfortable frame house which had been Jefferson Burdick's home at the time of his death.

The house was almost new, sturdy, and well painted without being elaborate. Burdick merely glanced at the living-accommodations, recognizing absently that this had been a matter of careful planning on the part of Uncle Jeff. Mostly he was interested in the cozy-looking front room which his uncle had equipped as an office. It had been this room which was headquarters for the various Burdick interests. In this room Jefferson Burdick had been murdered.

A side window opened upon a narrow yard where flowers bloomed. Doctor Burdick crossed the room to look out, noting the hard-packed clay path below the window. It was easy to see how the killer could have committed his deed without leaving a trace.

Clay seemed to make an effort at taking the attention away from the past tragedy. "If I were you," he suggested conversationally, "I'd move right in. You'll have comfortable sleeping-accommodations here and you can still take your meals at Kennicott's. In that way you can study papers and records at your leisure."

"Good idea," Burdick replied. "Although I'm not looking forward to much leisure. I want to get this thing cleaned up—and fast."

He was on his way back to the Valley House for his scanty belongings, dodging people who demanded news of the shooting-scrape, when he saw Sheriff Hickey and his posse riding in. A single glance told him that Dillingham was not with the lawmen but that the tin trunk had been recovered. Instantly he turned to aim for the sheriff's office, a renewed sense of anger nagging at him. So Dillingham had fallen victim to the unknown enemy! For the moment Burdick could forget that the fellow had been practically a crook; just now he was thinking of a friendly sort of individual who had been unlucky enough to be mistaken for Frank Burdick. Apparently the mistake had been fatal for Dillingham.

The thought made him pretty sober as he greeted Hickey. The sheriff's face was tired, even through the whiskers, and he shook his head in answer to Burdick's question.

"Never caught sight of 'em, Frank. Found your trunk back in a gulch near the north end of the canyon country but no sign of anybody movin'. Ed claims the bandits holed up fer a spell last evenin', then went on deeper into the hills. It musta been last night that they busted open the trunk. Then they left it this mornin'. No tellin' how much stuff youh'll find missin'."

"No trace of Dillingham?"

"Nope. Seems like they collared onto him fer keeps."

They talked it over at some length while Hickey and two of his deputies unsaddled. On the lawman's part there wasn't much more to tell; he had already summed it up pretty well. Burdick reported the events of the day in Osage and up the river, then asked suddenly, "Did you happen to take a look at the bundle Dillingham had on the stage?"

"Sure. I went over last evenin'. Thought I might git an idea by seein' what kinda luggage the pore critter had."

"Any luck?"

Hickey frowned. "I ain't figgered it out yet. That bundle didn't have a danged thing in it but dirty clothes, some empty bottles, some odd papers, and about a quart o' the worst licker I ever tried to swaller."

Burdick smiled in spite of his sense of tragedy. "It answers my question," he commented. "Dillingham was the harmless fraud he claimed to be. Now I'm sure he was seized in mistake for me."

Chapter Nine

THE REMAINDER OF THE AFTERNOON was a busy time for Doctor Burdick. He followed Lawyer Clay's advice and moved into the Burdick home, getting the recovered trunk delivered there and learning that his instruments were all in good order although several articles of clothing had been taken by the bandits. It was better luck than he had expected.

After that he made a call upon Bob Davies. Ellen's father was a man who didn't look his fifty years. He was slender, a little stooped from much working at a bench, but his face was unlined and his eyes were the same shade of keen blue that Burdick had noticed in the girl. More important, he was cordial, something Burdick had not expected.

"Glad to have you back, Frank," he greeted, his voice the husky whisper which had always been characteristic of him. "We've been hearin' a lot about yo' today. Seems like some of us had a wrong idea. Turpin's been explainin'."

Burdick smiled. "Lucky for me I managed to get a newspaper man to believe me. Maybe folks won't be so hard on me when they know the facts."

"I reckon not. Me, I'm kinda ashamed that I thought the way I did."

"No hard feelings. It must have looked bad." He let the conversation run on long enough to determine that Turpin had really given good publicity to the true facts. Then he said, "Maybe you can help to give me a lead. The man who tried to get me the other night in Butte was clumsy. I took his gun away from him—and it's got a Diamond K on it. I thought maybe you'd be able to trace it. You've always done a bit of business with the men in this basin."

Davies nodded interestedly, and Burdick produced the forty-five he had taken from the stocky holdup man. Instantly the gunsmith's eyes opened wide.

"Gosh, Frank! I believe I know this gun. Let me take a look at my ledger book."

He leafed through the volume for a minute or two, studying several entries. Then he turned back, a puzzled frown on the thin features. "I bought that gun nearly two years ago. From a cowboy who'd been working for Lowry at Diamond K. That's probably when the brand was scratched on it. This buckaroo was headin' East, or so he claimed, and wanted money. I bought the gun cheap because it had a bad trigger action. I repaired it and had it here in the shop for over a year. Then I sold it just last March."

"Who bought it?" The question was sharp, almost harsh.

Davies's face made it clear that he knew the letdown Burdick was going to get from his answer. "Your uncle bought it. I remember him saying that he wanted to have an extra gun on hand."

"But he didn't say why?"

"No. If he did I don't recall it."

Burdick turned abruptly, disappointed at having the promising lead fizzle out in a new puzzle. "Thanks," he said shortly.

As he left the shop he saw Sam Kennicott and Ellen Davies coming in from upriver but he didn't wait to talk with them. Instead he went into Proctor's store and bought a quantity of provisions. He was mildly pleased to note that the dour proprietor seemed to have softened a little, evidently under the influence of Turpin's explanations, but Burdick did not push matters. For the moment he was concerned only with finding time to do some thinking. Taking up residence in Uncle Jeff's home and doing his own cooking might help those thoughts a little.

No one came to interrupt him and when he finally went to bed in the huge double bed which had been his uncle's he had made a careful list of all the facts he knew. A second list enumerated facts subject to doubt. A third list was made up of the pertinent questions demanding answers. It was the third list that represented a sort of work schedule. Somehow he had to find those answers.

1.—*Why was Jefferson Burdick killed when he was generally known to be dying?*
2.—*What happened to Dillingham after the stage bandits discarded the trunk?*
3.—*Who intercepted the mail?*
4.—*Why did the stocky man in Butte attempt murder when the outlaws on the stage robbery went to the trouble of kidnaping?*
5.—*What do the Lowrys really want in this basin?*
6.—*Who was back of the attack at the Big Hole Saloon?*
7.—*How did Uncle Jeff's gun get into the hands of the bandit in Butte?*

There were many other questions he might have added to the list but he did not bother to put them in writing. Some of them were connected with the questions in the list; others were so clear in his mind that he didn't need to write them. For example, he wanted to know several things about both Ellen Davies and Mark Clay. He wanted to know whether the bank and stage company records were straight. He even wanted a little more information on the matter of Doc Dolan's blunder.

Finally he slept but the questions were in his thoughts again when he opened his eyes to a new day. He deliberately took his time in getting breakfast, trying to make himself slow down in hope that he could set his mind a good example and restrain its furious pace. He was still trying when Mark Clay and Ellen Davies appeared for a continuation of the conference which had been interrupted on the previous day. There was only a brief mention of the shooting affair, then the three of them set about the task of summarizing the various facts about Jefferson Burdick's estate.

The attorney remained long enough to complete his statement of accounting, then left the routine work of handling details to Ellen Davies. In the next two hours Burdick probed grimly into every tiny angle, learning little that he could connect with the death of his uncle but getting a very clear impression that Miss Davies knew her work with a remarkable thoroughness.

Finally he broke into the endless series of questions and answers, pointing to the clock on the wall. "Time to stop and eat. Now answer me one question that's not in the books. Who do you think killed my uncle?"

Her features were expressionless as she countered, "Are you really so much concerned?"

"I am. Believe me. I know you've put me down as a fortune hunter who didn't care about anything until there was money to be had. I can't prove that you're wrong about me and I don't quite blame you for feeling that way. Just give me the benefit of the doubt long enough to go along with that question. It's more important to me than any of the rest of this."

"Very well. I'm almost convinced. After watching you yesterday and hearing the story they're telling around town I'm— Well, it seems likely that you're just what you claim."

He grimaced a little. "A grudging sort of endorsement but better than none. While you're feeling charitable answer my question."

She almost smiled—but didn't. "I don't know the answer. You must understand that I admired your uncle more than anyone I ever knew. I've racked my brain trying to figure out who could have been so brutal. I simply don't know."

"Have you considered the fact that my uncle was generally believed to be dying?"

"Of course. That's why it seemed so completely useless that he should have been murdered. Even a thorough villain doesn't risk a murder if it can be avoided."

"Then you realize that his killer must have been some-

one who had to take that risk—or someone who thought
he had to."

"Apparently."

"Then we've narrowed the field quite a bit. Yesterday
we talked about the number of people—including yourself—who stood to gain something by my uncle's death.
So far as I can see every one of them would have been
content to wait a few days, weeks or even months for
nature to take its course. And every one of them must
have known the open secret that my uncle was a dying
man. Only someone pressed for time or someone ignorant
of the state of Uncle Jeff's health would have resorted to
murder at that particular time."

To his surprise she looked around with eyes that be-
trayed something like horror. "I didn't think—"

"Go on. What didn't you think?"

She seemed to pull herself together with an effort. "Very
well. We're being completely frank. Let me remind you
where you stand in this. No one in Osage knows just where
you were at the time of your uncle's death. Since you had
not heard anything from him you didn't know about his
condition." She didn't elaborate on the implication. She
didn't need to.

For a moment Burdick was almost too surprised to
speak. Then he shook his head slowly. "I'm afraid I'll
have to explode that one for you. I can account for almost
every minute of my time during the entire week in which
the tragedy took place. Completing a professional education involves quite a lot, you know. I was busy all the
time and in the company of quite a few people."

"Then you'd better get evidence to prove your statement," she told him. "When people begin to figure this
out the way you've just done they'll start jumping at conclusions the way I did."

He decided that the remark was intended to be helpful.
Evidently she had changed her mind about him even to
the point where she was accepting his word without proof.
At least for the present.

"Meanwhile I'll go on with my probing," he told her. "And that's where you can help. I want you to try some detailed thinking. See if you can recall every little detail of your contacts with Uncle Jeff over the past few months. Tell me who came to call on him, who had business dealings with him. Try to recall whether he showed any unusual worry—beyond his own critical condition, of course. Were any strangers around during that time, particularly within the last week or so of his life?"

She sat up a little straighter. "You remind me of something right there. Your uncle was handling some kind of deal just before his death, a deal which he refused to tell me about. On every other matter I handled even supposedly secret details but on this one he wouldn't even tell me who the man was."

"What man?"

"The man who called on him twice. The first time I saw him was about ten days before your uncle's death. The second time was only hours before he was killed."

"Can you describe him?"

"Roughly. I never saw him closely. He was short, very heavy-bodied, and dark. He wore a mustache but no beard, I think. I took him for a prospector but that was only a guess."

"Any circumstances to make the visits seem unusual?"

"Only that your uncle ignored my hints and wouldn't talk about him. As far as I could see the man simply dropped in and went away again. There was no excitement, no threats, nothing. I mentioned the matter to Sheriff Hickey when he was investigating and I think he made some effort to trace the man. At least he mentioned to me that the lead had petered out. I'm afraid I didn't consider the matter as being very important; I was too disturbed over the obvious theory that the killer had been someone—someone like myself—with something to gain."

Suddenly he realized what a strain she had been under during the past weeks. In a way her position was somewhat similar to his own. She had been on the list of suspects even though the tragedy had been something pretty personal to her.

"I'll talk to Hickey," he said gently. "Now try to see if you can come up with anything else."

She shook her head. "It's hopeless, I'm afraid. I've already thought and thought. There just wasn't anything else."

"Very well. Let's talk about something else. Would you be willing to go back to work, for me as you once did for my uncle?"

"Well, I don't know how—"

"Aren't the wages satisfactory?"

"Quite. Your uncle was most generous. It's just that I wasn't intending to keep on working." She blushed a little as she said it, and he remembered the big hoeman she had given the extra attention out there at Fishel's.

"It won't be a permanent arrangement," he explained. "I have no intention of remaining in Osage. As soon as convenient I wish to start practice in a community of somewhat larger size. Temporarily, however, I'm stuck here. This estate must be settled and I'm determined to track down my uncle's killer." He hesitated a moment before adding, "There's also another matter. Doc Dolan's not going to last long. I had a pretty good look at him yesterday and I read his notes. I think he's dying of the cancer he believed Uncle Jeff had. Those periodic sprees of his have been getting worse because he's in constant pain."

Her look of horror changed swiftly as she grasped the added implication. "Do you infer that your uncle didn't have what Doctor Dolan thought he did?"

"I'm sure he didn't. But we won't talk about it now. That's water under the bridge. Just now I'm thinking of the days when Dolan meant a great deal to me. I'd like to stick around and help him through his last days. There won't be many of them, I'm sure. By that time we'll have the estate cleaned up and maybe I'll accomplish my other purpose. Will you help?"

"It's a deal," she said quietly.

He smiled briefly. "With extra pay for nursing, of course."

This time he got a smile in return. It made him feel better. For the first time he knew the satisfaction of a real ally. Turpin and Kennicott might be friendly enough but somehow he had a lot more confidence in the ability of this quiet young woman who had scorned him so openly but had decided to trust him after all.

"Now I'm inviting you to lunch," he said. "I owe you that for your efforts to date—and I owe it to myself after the breakfast I prepared."

"We'd be smarter to have lunch here," she countered. "I noticed that you had secured some supplies and I'll do the honors. In that way we can get on with the work."

"Anxious to get it over, are you?" he bantered. "Won't that big freckle-faced hoeman wait for you?"

"He'll have to," she retorted, on her way to the kitchen.

He followed her part way, dropping the brief humor. "I'm going to write a letter—if you think you can get along in the kitchen without me. Sing out when you're ready."

He entered the kitchen without a summons, carrying a letter in his hand. Miss Davies looked up, offering a trace of a smile. "I was just about to call," she told him.

"Nice timing. By the way, has our benevolent federal government ever gotten around to establishing postal service in the basin?"

She shook her head. "No. The stage company still takes mail both ways. They run lock boxes on all coaches and take care of the posting of letters in both Butte and Salt Lake."

"What about postage? Any particular way that's handled?"

"Just as it used to be. Stroud will charge you a fee that includes the proper stamp." Then she looked up with a half-frown. "Probably you'll rate free mail service. Your uncle always sent his without fees."

He read the meaning behind her almost too casual remark. "You're guessing correctly," he told her. "The letter is to the hospital authorities in Chicago. I'm asking them to send an affidavit to prove that I was in that city on the tenth day of June. Incidentally, I'm getting information on mail handling in an attempt to decide who did the tampering. As of right now it looks like a dead heat between you and Virgil Stroud. Either of you could have done the trick and both of you had good reason to keep me away from here."

She replaced the plate she had just picked up from the table. "Are you implying that I—"

"Take it easy. I'm just pointing out that I have as good reason to distrust you as you have to distrust me. I have to keep it in mind even though I'm about settled on Stroud as the guilty party."

She relaxed a little. "Do you think Stroud killed your uncle?"

"On that point I'm not even ready to guess. I simply think Stroud had the best opportunity to be the mail meddler. Beyond that I don't go—yet."

They lunched in almost complete silence, speaking only on the few occasions when Burdick complimented the girl on her food preparations. Then she went back to the office chores and he headed for the stage station.

The early-afternoon sun was warm but the air had a slight chill in it as a light north wind swept down across the divide. More than the crispness, however, Burdick noticed the slightly acrid odor. For a minute or two he was puzzled but then he realized why the scent was vaguely familiar. It was the smell of a distant copper plant. That north wind was bringing smelter fumes down from Anaconda way. Even with the miles intervening the odor was annoying, not only because it was unpleasant but because it was a sort of symbol of what mining did to a pleasant country.

The thought occurred to him that mineral wealth was not an unmixed blessing any way it appeared. Maybe the ravaging of nature had to have its revenge but it always seemed that the country or region producing the wealth was never the one to gain by it. The big gains went elsewhere, and the mining towns became dirty, forlorn communities full of unhappy people. Always there was the excitement of fabulous prospects but then the place bred its quota of disaster and violence, finally collapsing entirely. Smoke on the range could be just as fatal to the cattle business and Burdick knew a quick hope that the copper strikes would not come nearer to the Big Hole Basin. It would be a shame to spoil good cattle country for the elusive benefits of a dubious future in mining.

His first stop was at Hickey's office but the lawman was not there. A scrawled note announced that he would not return until the following day. Burdick guessed the sheriff was hunting bandits or Lowry gunmen—and he had a hunch it was the latter.

On another hunch he crossed the street to the combination feed store and livery stable which Hickey used almost as a secondary headquarters. Whispering Wilson, its squat, bowlegged proprietor, was practically a deputy, supplying mounts when real deputies were drawn into service and generally acting as local contact man for the sheriff. He might know something of the lawman's activities.

"Howdy, Whisper," Burdick greeted him. "Got a bronc for me as good as the one Kennicott hired yesterday?"

"All good broncs in my place," Wilson retorted, his voice the same old murmur of secrecy. Burdick knew that the man had talked that way ever since an accident which had injured his vocal cords but he always had the impression that he was engaged in some dark conspiracy when he conversed with Wilson.

"They ought to be," he said, smiling. "All stolen from the best ranches in Montana."

Wilson did not take offense. It was a standing joke. "I got a legal bill of sale for every danged one of 'em," he confided.

"Sure. Why not? You stand in with Hickey. Every time he runs down a horse thief with a good bronc he sees to it that you get the first chance to buy the critter from the county. It's a real graft if I ever heard of one."

Both men laughed. Despite the age of the legend—and its basic truth—it was still considered as first-class humor in Osage.

"Have a nag ready about two-thirty," Burdick went on. "I want to ride out and look at that fellow Fishel. And by the way, do you know when Tex will be back? I've got a couple of questions I want to fire at him."

"He's upriver on that shootin' scrape. Didn't figger to git back till tomorrow but mebbe yuh'll run into him up there."

"Possibly. But maybe you can help me out on one point. You always know more about Hickey than he knows about himself. I understand that after my uncle was killed Tex got interested in a stocky *hombre* who'd been seen around town that day. Do you know whether he ever located the jasper?"

"Sure he did. But it didn't pan out much good."

"No?"

"No good at all, I reckon. Tex traced him to Kennicott's bar and from there to the stage station. Sam remembered him as a jigger lookin' fer a grubstake, and Stroud claimed he'd let him work his way back to Butte as helper on a freight wagon."

"When did he leave town?"

"About two hours before yuhr uncle was shot. Tex made plenty certain on that point. The driver of the wagon swore to it."

"Did Tex ever find out what the man wanted of my uncle?"

"Nope. Kennicott thought it musta been a grubstake job, same as with him."

"Do you remember which driver he went with?"

"Nope. Sorry."

Burdick let it go at that. With the prospect of an unpleasant interview at the stage station ahead of him he didn't want to let his thoughts go too far afield. The meeting with Virgil Stroud was going to be one in which he would need all his powers of concentration.

Chapter Ten

AT THE STAGE STATION Burdick walked in on a tense scene. Question-Mark Turpin was leaning across the barrier which separated office from waiting-room, his nose barely two inches from the red face of Virgil Stroud who was leaning across from the opposite side. It was obvious that they had been indulging in a bit of acid conversation, and Stroud's testy voice was completing a bald threat.

"—a word o' that in yer dirty yella sheet and I'll take a bullwhip to ye!"

"Bring a gun with you!" Turpin snapped.

Burdick slammed the door behind him, its crash startling the belligerent pair out of their pose. It was Virgil Stroud who recovered first. His bony face was still red from the argument and it was clear that he was no less angry toward Frank Burdick. Taking a half-step away from Turpin he snarled, "This sounds like some of your talk, Frank! Turpin's been accusin' me of holdin' up the mails so as to keep ye from havin' words with yer uncle."

"I was about ready to make the same accusation," Burdick told him calmly. "At least I'd like to hear your explanation."

"Explanation be damned! I ain't lettin' no sneakin' skunk git out of his own responsibilities by tryin' to hang a thing like that on me!"

"Easy with the pet names, Virgil," Burdick warned, still calm. "You'll only convince people that you have something to hide. I've been looking into this mail situation and you seem to be the fellow who's right square in the middle. Got anything to say for yourself?"

"Why should I? You're not the law. You're not even my boss, even if ye did inherit yer uncle's property. I'm a partner in this business, ye know."

"You're a partner in a business subject to the law regarding settlement of estates," Burdick corrected. "As executor of that estate I can sew up every angle of the business if I feel that you're not fit to run it. At the moment I'm entertaining strong doubts."

"So that's yer game, hey?" Stroud rumbled. "Goin' to rawhide me to save yer own hide. Then I'm doin' some talkin', too! Mebbe folks might git to wonderin' where ye happened to be when yer uncle got shot."

Burdick saw that Turpin was looking up in some amazement. Evidently that possibility had not occurred to the newspaperman.

He pulled the letter from his inside pocket, showing it to the two men. "Someone else hinted at that accusation," he said, still keeping his voice down. "This letter is a request for affidavits which will prove my presence in Chicago continuously for a period of about three days. From the ninth to the eleventh, inclusive. How would you recommend that I send the letter so that it will not be subject to the interference we've been talking about?"

"All mail handled the regular way," Stroud said stiffly. "Two-bits cash. This'll be posted in Butte tomorrow night."

Burdick handed over a twenty-five cent piece and the letter. "You're witness to this, Turpin," he said shortly. Then, to Stroud: "Sure you don't want to talk about mail interference, Virgil? It might be easier to have your say now than to a postal inspector sometime later."

Stroud seemed to have lost a little of his belligerence. "Why try to hang it on me?" he demanded querulously. "I ain't the only one handled your uncle's letters. That Davies gal coulda done it."

"What about the stage driver? Did the same man always handle the mail sack?"

"Sure. It was always Slats McGill. He's been on the Butte run without a miss fer three years or more."

"Box always locked?"

"Yep. But McGill mighta—"

"Who handled it at the other end?"

"The Butte agent."

"Who was that?"

"Lane was there till about a year ago. Then we had a man named Calloway but he only lasted three or four months. Since then we had three agents, finally puttin' Lane back on the job about three weeks ago."

"That's interesting." He shot a significant glance at Turpin as he added, "The editor's anxious to make a yarn of this, Virgil. I heard you warn him not to print something or other. Maybe you'd prefer to tell him what you want the public to believe."

"I'll tell him nothin'!" Stroud almost bellowed. "All I'm sayin' is that I shipped yer uncle's mail every time it was left with me. And I'll swear no letters from you have been in the mail fer a couple o' years!"

"That's exactly the statement I wanted to hear," Burdick told him. "Now I'll leave you. Better get your books ready for inspection. As executor of the estate I'm planning to look them over tomorrow morning."

Turpin hurried after him as he went back to the street. There was a puzzled frown on the editor's still-red face. "Why did you let him talk you out of that hole he was in, Frank?" he asked. "I was trying to trap him into something when you busted in. I think he's guilty as hell."

Burdick smiled thinly. "Of course he is. He just admitted it."

"What?"

"Figure it out. He has practically admitted guilt and at the same time given me several new things to think about. By his own statement we know that several different agents have been in the Butte office. It seems impossible that every one of them should have been a party to the mail interference, yet letters were intercepted during the period when Butte agents changed frequently. So the interference didn't take place east of here. In the same way we can eliminate Miss Davies as a suspect. Stroud admits that he passed on no mail from me. I'll have to talk with the postmaster in Butte and I'll try to get a line on some

of those short-term stage agents who were in the Butte
office but it's already clear enough to satisfy me. Stroud's
the lad who held up the mail."

"Why?"

"It's reasonably clear, isn't it? He was trying to get
something for himself by stirring up hard feeling between
Uncle Jeff and me. I would guess that the terms of Uncle
Jeff's will were precisely what Virgil was aiming for."

"Then you think he killed your uncle?"

"That part's not so clear. He probably figured that I'd
be out here as soon as my work in Chicago was done and
he didn't want any of this to come out. Maybe he thought
Uncle Jeff was living too long to make his scheme safe."

"Sounds possible. Can you prove it?"

"No. I'm almost inclined to doubt it."

"Then what?"

"I don't know—and just now I don't have time to think
about it. I'm on my way to see a patient. Keep your ears
open and maybe you'll find some answers that I can't pick
up."

"Right," Turpin assured him. "I'll be lookin'."

He found a thin little girl of perhaps fourteen years in
charge at Fishel's. Too old for her age she was typical of
the working children of the frontier but at the moment
Doctor Burdick was glad to have it so. The child's early
assumption of responsibility might have been hard on
youthful exuberance but it had given her a steadiness
which made her capable of handling this chore.

"How's our patient, nurse?" he greeted. "I suppose you
are Miss Poor?"

"Bigelow," she corrected. "Sadie Bigelow. Charlie Bigelow's my pappy." Her tired grin indicated that she was
mighty pleased at being addressed as nurse.

"Bigelow?" he repeated. "Then your father is one of
the brothers who live upstream."

"That's right. Dave Bigelow is my uncle. He's the one
what's sweet on Ellen Davies. Lucky fer us, too, Pap says.

Ellen done a heap fer us in gettin' old Jeff Burdick to go on our paper." She blushed suddenly as though realizing that the man who had appeared in her mind solely as a physician was also the new holder of the mortgages which meant so much to her folks.

Burdick tried to put her at ease. "I guess Mr. Burdick knew what was good business. How's the patient?"

She motioned toward the bedroom. "He's kinda dopey yet. Uncle Dave stayed till Fishel got done bein' sick from the ether. This mornin' I made some beef broth. He swallowed a bit of it and he's been sleepin' ever since."

"Excellent. Sounds like he's been in very good hands."

Her smile broke out again, and he patted her thin shoulder as he went past into the other room. "I'll need hot water, nurse," he said gravely. "The dressings will have to be changed."

He found the wounded man much as the girl had stated, still sufficiently dazed from shock and pain so that he wasn't clear in his head. For a few minutes Fishel tried to talk but then he fainted, permitting the dressing change to be made without the discomfort which might have been expected. It was just as the job was being completed that they heard a rider come into the yard.

Sadie Bigelow went out, and presently Burdick could hear the sound of feminine voices in the kitchen. The new voice was vaguely familiar but he didn't stop to investigate, finishing his work before going into the other room.

Somewhat to his surprise it was Jane Lowry who greeted him. She looked a little harassed, even with her quick smile, and he realized that she had not been accepted with any cordiality by the Bigelow girl. The frown on the thin features of the child was eloquent enough.

"Good afternoon, Doctor," Miss Lowry greeted. "I hope you're not going to bark at me the way your assistant did."

Sadie looked up grimly. "She's a Lowry. It was her folks what shot up Fishel. She ain't got no call to come snoopin' around here."

Jane Lowry uttered a little laugh. "Damned before I

can say a word," she complained. "Actually I came because I want to know a few things—and because I'd like to help."

"Precious little help we'll git from a Lowry!" the younger girl snapped.

Miss Lowry shrugged. "You see, Doctor? It's very hard to live down a prejudice."

"Murderous shooting attempts go beyond the confines of prejudice," Burdick commented. "If Lowry riders were responsible for the wire-cutting and for the shooting of Ned Fishel I'd be inclined to sympathize with the feelings Sadie has just expressed."

"*If* Lowry riders did it," she repeated. "That's what I want to know. Sheriff Hickey was at our place this morning, asking questions which hinted that he entertained suspicions. My father didn't even know about this shooting and Rusty Aiken insists that none of our men were in this part of the basin at the time it happened. Both of them were pretty angry at having our boys accused."

"But you weren't satisfied? You came over to find out a few things for yourself. Is that it?"

She looked a little uncomfortable. "Sometimes it doesn't pay to take too much for granted. I'm sure my father and Rusty would not countenance violence but I remembered what happened in Osage the other evening. Our riders made an attack upon you—and they haven't been found to make explanations. I want to know what's going on."

"I'll certainly join you in that. Do you suspect anything in particular?"

"No. I simply want to know. What's more, I want to do something for the injured man. I've had some practical experience in nursing and I'm a neighbor, whether these folks want to accept me as such or not."

"Nursing seems to be quite a skill around here," he commented. "Miss Davies exhibited some aptitude in that line."

"You don't sound very cordial, I must say."

"Sorry. It's just that I'm surprised. However, I'm sure your offer will be gratefully accepted. This man is seriously injured and he'll need competent care for some time to come."

"I kin take care of him enough." Sadie Bigelow glowered.

"Then I'll be your helper," Miss Lowry proposed, her smile coming quickly as she turned to the sullen youngster. "Honestly, I'd like to help."

"You're Lowry," the girl insisted.

Burdick intervened. "It seems to me, Sadie, that we can use all the help we can get. How would it be if Miss Lowry took charge during the day until the danger is over? Then you could stand watch at night and nobody would be overworked."

It took some convincing but finally they worked out the details. Jane Lowry was to ride over from Diamond K each morning, assuming charge of the injured man for the day and leaving before sundown. Then Sadie Bigelow would go on duty. Barring bad weather it would be a workable arrangement, one which Burdick liked the more he thought of it. Fishel would profit by the care, there would be a chance for the opposing cattle interests to find some common ground of understanding—and the attendant physician would have an added interest in making a daily trip upriver.

Miss Lowry had come prepared to stay for some hours so they persuaded the Bigelow girl to go home for a bit of rest, hinting that she might like to tell her folks about the new arrangement. They watched her ride awkwardly out of sight, then Miss Lowry turned to stare worriedly at Burdick. "Are these people really so bitter against us, Doctor? Do you think our men really did this?"

Burdick shook his head. "Yes to the first question. I don't know about the second. It's one of the puzzles I'm bothered about, maybe one of the most important ones."

"You mean you are concerned?"

"I'm beginning to think so. When I first stuck my head into this mess I thought it was complicated enough with at least three people having a good reason for trying to keep me out of the basin. Now I'm afraid the trouble is even deeper than I suspected."

She waited for him to explain but instead he started to give instructions about the care of the wounded man. She listened carefully, asking the practical questions which told him that she had not exaggerated in claiming to have some skill in nursing. It struck him as a remarkable coincidence that two such charming young women as Jane Lowry and Ellen Davies should turn up in the same region, both of them outstandingly sure of themselves and both so capable along the same sort of lines.

Then he heard a stir of movement from the other room. Signing for the girl to follow him he went in and found Fishel's eyes open, a spark of understanding showing through.

"Feeling better?" he asked.

"Hard to tell," a weak voice replied. "Yo' Doc Burdick?"

"That's right."

"Seems like I heard somebody call yo' that. Thanks fer helpin'."

"Glad to. Think you can handle a bit of broth?"

"Mebbe. I'll try."

"Fine. Miss Lowry is going to spell your other nurse for a while. She'll take good care of you."

Fishel stared. "Lowry? That's—"

"Say it," the girl cut in. "I want to know."

There was a dull silence before the wounded man muttered, "I figgered it was Lowry riders what— Never mind. I'm right happy folks wanta help." He shut his eyes again, evidently having said all he intended to say.

Burdick nodded toward the girl. "Better see about the broth. I think there is some on the stove."

In the kitchen he asked, "Are you sure you're willing to stay? This might get awkward."

"I'll stay," she told him. "For a number of reasons."

"Good. Also for a number of reasons. I'll be out again tomorrow."

For just a moment she caught his eye, evidently trying

to read his thoughts as he must have read hers. Then she looked away and went on with her self-imposed task. Burdick delayed only long enough to give full instructions about care of wounded men in the event of emergency, then he went out, content to let matters rest the way they were.

He rode thoughtfully, trying to make up his mind about the puzzling yet intriguing situation he had left behind him. As he had told Jane Lowry he was beginning to smell a complication which he had not even suspected at first. As yet he could find no definite relation between the rumblings of approaching range war and the attacks upon himself but he had a solid hunch that such a link existed. It was much like the business of the intercepted letters and the murder of Jefferson Burdick. There simply had to be a connection. Otherwise none of this nasty mess made sense.

Stopping to open the gate in Fishel's wire broke his concentration and made him notice the strong odor of sulphur in the continuing northerly breeze. The acrid scent had been in his nostrils since noon but now he suddenly realized that it was stronger.

For a moment he knew only annoyance but then he realized that there was no evident reason why the fumes should be more powerful here than in Osage. This part of the basin was farther away from Butte and at least as far from Anaconda. He estimated that neither town could be less than thirty miles by direct line from Osage. Quite a distance for an odor like that to persist.

It was then that he began to scan the rugged slopes which towered above him on the north and west. The valley floor was of no great width at that particular point, the river making a bend close in toward the first abrupt climb which might be construed as a foothill. Beyond that first ridge, Burdick knew, was rough country, a series of broken draws, steep grades, and ragged, irregular canyons. He had ridden those canyons often enough in search of straying stock and he knew that it was the one place in this part of the basin where prospectors had been active. Dog Robber Gulch and Reveille Canyon had both silver and copper prospect holes although none had ever reported success.

The afternoon sun was already dropping behind the high peaks to the west, throwing long, irregular shadows across the northern slopes to make every outline deceptive. Trying to spot detail on that rugged upsweep of gray-green patchwork was like trying to see a squatting jack rabbit in a mesquite clump. The eye insisted on being fooled.

Still Burdick fancied that he could detect a faint wisp of smoke back there at the base of the big rise. He knew that he might be looking at a bare place on the mountain but the sight still brought a start. Interesting possibilities flooded into his mind and he turned the bronc's head without hesitation, sending the animal up the steep climb which would take him to the top of the first bench.

From that point he could still see the light patch against the dark mountain but the afternoon was rapidly dying and he could not distinguish any more detail than he had been able to do from the riverbank.

Directly in front of him lay another sharp climb but this one he knew to be a long, sharp ridge which masked the real slope of the Continental Divide. Long ago it had been named Hardtack Ridge, probably by the same ex-doughfoot who had given the title of Reveille Canyon to the steep but shallow valley which lay behind it and Dog Robber Gulch to the single cut which broke through the ridge and gave access to the canyon. Burdick decided that there would be more profit in taking a look at the gulch than in trying to race approaching darkness for a better look at the supposed smoke.

He met no one as he let the horse angle up the easy grade toward the mouth of Dog Robber Gulch but the ground in front of him was worthy of study. Someone had been doing quite a bit of riding up here on the bench. He read the sign with care, deciding that as many as a dozen men had ridden toward the mouth of the gulch while some four or five had gone in the other direction. Or maybe he was studying the tracks of men who had come and gone over the same trail. That would mean fewer men but more frequent travel, in either case a significant bit of sign.

He considered the possibility that Hickey's posse might have made the tracks but quickly discarded the theory. The sheriff had done his investigating from a different angle and had turned back toward town after losing the trail back there in the canyons to the northwest. It seemed likely that Hickey and his deputies had not been near this end of Hardtack Ridge. The conclusion made him sorry that he was unarmed. It wasn't likely that he would meet any friends up here.

It was getting pretty dark when he approached the mouth of Dog Robber Gulch but there was still enough light for him to see the wheel ruts which marked a well-beaten trail into the opening. Heavy wagons had come and gone within the past few days, following other ruts which indicated that there had been some volume of traffic through the cut. There was just time for him to realize that the wagons must have come up the grade from the general direction of Calamity Rock, when his speculations were interrupted violently by the whining slug which passed over his head.

Distantly, from somewhere near the top of Hardtack Ridge, he heard the slap of a rifle. Then he took the hint and sent the bronc at a run down the line of the wagon tracks. There was no point in offering himself as a target for even long-distance shooting. Anyway, he had learned enough to give him a lead on what he suspected was the key to the whole puzzle. Time enough to argue with that rifleman when there was daylight overhead and a gun in his hand.

Chapter Eleven

DARKNESS WAS FULL upon the basin when he rode into Osage but he had a feeling that light was beginning to break in his own mind. For the first time he was not trying to fight shadows. All those conflicting details were beginning to fit into a neat pattern of calculated villainy. He still didn't know exactly who was holding the cards against him but he had a pretty good idea of what kind of cards had been dealt. Now he had to figure how to draw so as to strengthen his own hand. It wasn't going to be easy but at least he wasn't riding blindfolded any longer.

As an added note of optimism he realized that the rifleman on Hardtack Ridge could not have recognized him in the gathering gloom. The shot had been merely a warning to a casual stranger who had displayed too much curiosity about those tracks. Probably the man on the ridge would pass a warning to his fellows but no one would be able to tell that it had been Frank Burdick who had been there at the mouth of the gulch. At least Burdick hoped it would be that way. He needed a little time to get some facts straight.

At the stable he managed to give Whispering Wilson a rather garrulous account of Fishel's condition, taking care to report the activities of Jane Lowry as volunteer nurse. It was evident that Wilson was assuming a connection between Miss Lowry's presence at the Fishel cabin and Burdick's belated return to town but Burdick was content to let it go at that. It saved explanations.

He was also content to meet no one as he headed for the building which he was already thinking of as home. Somehow the idea seemed pleasant even though he still persisted in his plan to open medical practice elsewhere.

There were sandwiches on the kitchen table and a pot of coffee on the stove ready for heating. The sight brought a smile to his almost grim features. For the second time in a few hours he was being reminded of the efficiency of a very charming young woman. Maybe it was a good thing he didn't propose to remain in Osage; it would be pretty tough to lose Ellen Davies now that she had made herself so important to him. For a moment he almost hated that freckled hoeman but then he laughed aloud, almost derisively. Better to keep thoughts like that out of mind. Both Ellen and Jane might be useful to him—and either one of them might prove to be enemies. A smart man had to remember it.

He spent the evening in a detailed study of the books Ellen had been working on during the afternoon. Some of it was dreary routine, giving him nothing more than a general picture of the way Uncle Jeff had conducted his business affairs, but here and there he picked up a piece of information which helped him to understand the underlying thread of intrigue. In no case did he find anything to alter the picture as he had begun to see it while several of the items offered corroborative evidence and added detail. When he finally crawled into bed he thought he knew most of the answers. Now the problem was one of identifying the men who were responsible. He didn't quite know how he was going to smoke them out but he determined to light plenty of fires—and quickly.

By the time Ellen Davies came to work next morning he had his plans pretty well perfected. Still he contrived to appear casual, thanking her for her culinary efforts of the previous day and reporting conditions at the Fishel place. She seemed surprised to hear of Jane Lowry's part in the matter but there was none of the resentment he had half expected.

"I don't imagine Jane knows half of the dirty work that goes on behind her back," she commented thoughtfully. "As far as that goes, I don't suppose her father knows, either. It's that crooked Rusty Aiken who's responsible."

"I understand Aiken has worked himself into the good graces of the Lowrys in more ways than one. Sam Kennicott told me he's expecting to marry Jane."

"Maybe he is," she said, her tone indicating that she didn't care to discuss the matter.

Burdick changed the subject, getting right down to business. "Today we light some fires," he announced, thinking of his plans of the previous evening. "Yesterday I told Stroud that we'd be down to check the stage company's

books but I'd prefer to have you handle the chore alone.
You certainly know more about it than I do and I'd like
to use the time elsewhere."

"Do you have authority to demand accounts?" she
asked. "I thought your executorship was inoperative until
the will was offered for probate."

He offered her a quizzical glance. "You sound like Mark
Clay and I suppose you've been talking to him."

"I have."

"Then forget about it. I didn't know of such a detail
and I don't think Stroud will know. We'll run a bluff
on him. If he objects it'll look suspicious and I don't believe he'll want that to happen."

"What are we looking for?" she inquired. "Some effort
to swindle you out of part of the estate?"

"Bother the estate! I'm looking for someone with a
motive to commit murder. There's probably a swindle
connected with it but I'm betting that the fraud would
have been against Uncle Jeff personally, not against the
estate."

"But you have no particular suspicions?"

"Sure I do. See if you can find evidence of company
wagons being used without a record of income. Also you
might check incoming shipments. I'd like to know whether
anyone has been buying unusual quantities of salt."

It gave him a sort of warped pleasure to see her astonishment. For the first time somebody beside Frank Burdick was getting a puzzle to think about.

After she had gone out he proceeded upon his own errands, getting a little extra pleasure out of surprising
Mark Clay and storekeeper Proctor with his questions.
Once Clay understood the nature of the queries he lost
his air of bewilderment and agreed to keep his own coun-
sel about the propriety of the authority Burdick was preparing to assume. Not so with Proctor. When Burdick
left the store, armed with the information that no one
had bought unusual quantities of salt from him, Proctor's
jaw was still slack.

He followed those two calls with a visit to the bank. Dan Whiteside met him effusively but with a nervousness of manner which caught Burdick's attention. He had known the little man for a number of years but now found it hard to realize that Whiteside had once been regarded as a pretty tough little rooster. Once he had operated freight wagons into Virginia City and Bannack, making money out of the trade in a day when a man had to be both tough and resourceful to stay alive. Now he had become almost a dandy, the sedentary life of a banker evidently having done something to him. His store teeth were white and even, his wig made him look almost like a clothing dummy, and his garments were just a shade too meticulous for belief, especially in a combination mining camp and cow town. The false smile fitted the rest of his appearance exactly.

"I've been expecting you ever since I heard you'd arrived in Osage," he announced, almost with his greeting. "Clay informed me that you'd be taking over executorship of the estate so I've tried to get everything ready for you. Actually the accounts are a bit out of order, you know. Your uncle ran things pretty much to suit himself, even though I was supposed to be in full charge. I never could get him to keep formal accounts."

That sounded like a bit of hedging, Burdick thought, but he kept his voice even as he remarked, "Likely to be that way, I suppose. However, I'm not coming to check books now. Miss Davies will do that, probably this afternoon. I just wanted to let you know that she will have full authority for the job."

The little banker's tiny features seemed to relax. Either he was relieved to be rid of Frank Burdick or he had a notion that it would be easier to fool Ellen Davies. One way or another he was hiding something, Burdick felt certain.

As though to cover the relief he feared was showing, Whiteside asked about Ned Fishel. It suited him well enough to change topics so Burdick told his story quietly, mentioning Jane Lowry's unexpected role.

Whiteside nodded. "She'd do that," he said. "I think the Lowrys are trying to run an honest cattle business and I never could see why there was so much hard feeling on the part of those nesters."

"Getting shot might be one good reason."

"But there's no proof that the Lowrys did it. I think there's something more behind it, something we don't know about."

Burdick looked him squarely in the eyes. "I think there's a lot about this town which is beneath the surface," he said. "I'm expecting to drag a lot of it to the surface in the near future—and a lot of folks are going to get hurt."

Again he knew that Whiteside was afraid. The man's relief had faded away to leave something like panic in his dark eyes. Burdick left it that way and started for the door. He was getting his fires lighted, all right; he could just hope that he wasn't dragging Ellen Davies into a spot where she would be the first one to get singed.

Tex Hickey was leading a bronc into Wilson's stable when Burdick came out on the street once more. Evidently the other members of the posse had gone to their various homes so Burdick went into the sheriff's office, waiting there until the bewhiskered lawman put in an appearance.

"What luck?" Burdick asked.

"None, dammit! I talked to Joe Lowry at Diamond K and he swears he ain't tryin' to bust up no fences. Rusty Aiken makes the same claim. Says there ain't been no Diamond K riders on that part of the range."

"You believe them?"

"Don't see no good reason not to, 'specially when I found Jane Lowry takin' care o' Fishel. She's a right smart gal, that one, and mighty purty, too. Seems like a young sawbones like yuhrself wouldn't find it too hard to take care of a feller when he had a nurse like that."

"I'm feeling no pain about it." Burdick grinned. "Did you talk to Fishel?"

"Shore. He don't know who he had the brush with. He

admits he fired first 'cause they was acuttin' his bobwire. He thinks one of 'em was forkin' a Diamond K hoss but he ain't sure."

"Did he tell you that while Jane Lowry was in the room?"

"Shore. She wouldn't let me git near him till I promised I wouldn't rile him none. Then she stuck with me to make shore I'd behave."

"Do you think Fishel held back to save her feelings?"

"Nope. I reckon he told me all he knowed."

"How's Miss Lowry making out with the other nesters? Some of 'em didn't like it much for her to take over, I imagine."

"She's got 'em eatin' outa her hand." Hickey chuckled. "But I got somethin' else to tell yuh. Yesterday I was back in the mountains to the west and I met a prospector who tole me that Loud Noyes was back in the hills."

"Noise?" Burdick echoed. "I smelled a stink but I didn't hear anything."

Hickey's laugh rumbled through the room. "I reckon Whisperin' didn't mention the name to yuh. He just tole me that yuh was askin' about the polecat. Noyes is the feller what was in town the day yuhr uncle got killed. 'Loud' Noyes they call him—fer some odd reason or other."

Burdick smiled at the humor but asked sharply, "What's the story on that fellow? I've got a hunch about him."

"I had one, too," the sheriff retorted, a little ruefully. "But it didn't turn up no color, just country rock. It seemed like kinda odd that he happened to be in town jest at that time so I follered him up mighty careful. Seems like he went to yer uncle and claimed to be a prospector lookin' fer a grubstake. He didn't git nowhere so he tried it on Kennicott. Still no dice. Then he musta decided to go back to Butte and work in the mines there. Leastways, that's how he handed it to Virgil Stroud. Virgil put him on as guard with a couple o' wagonloads of green hides and he left Osage late that same afternoon. Billy McCandless was driver and he claims Noyes went all the way to Butte with him and was never out of his sight."

"Then Noyes would have been several miles from Osage at the time my uncle was killed?"

"Seems like. Anyway we didn't have no way to tie Noyes up with yuhr uncle—and it seems mighty certain that Jeff Burdick was killed by somebody what knew him and had somethin' to gain by the killin'."

"Maybe there was such a connection. Can you describe Noyes for me?"

"Secondhand. He was about five-eight or less but built heavy all the way down. Musta weighed in at around two hundred. Bull neck, big paws, and powerful-lookin'. Swarthy-complected, they tell me. Why?"

"That's a pretty good description of the man I saw at the stage office in Butte, the man who tried to kill me at the Copper King Hotel."

Hickey shook his head. "Plenty of tough, stocky men in this country."

"But that isn't all. I took a gun from that man when he was trying a bit of rough stuff on the street. The gun had a Diamond K carved on its butt. Bob Davies told me he sold that gun to Uncle Jeff a few months ago."

"Gosh! That makes it look different."

"And that's not all. This fellow Noyes didn't visit my uncle for the first time on the day you've been investigating. Ellen says he was there about a week or ten days earlier. Uncle Jeff wouldn't tell her what kind of a deal he had with the man so it must have been more than just a prospecting proposition."

Hickey was sitting up straight now. "Gosh again! What d'yuh make of it?"

"From where I sit it looks like there's been a lot of plain and fancy lies told in this town. You have to take everything you hear with a pinch of salt—which reminds me, who's been buying a lot of salt lately?"

The whiskers parted as Hickey's jaw dropped. "What?" he gulped.

"Salt. Who's been buying it in big quantities? No, I'm not crazy. I want to know."

"Ask Stroud. He freights it in. I'd guess the Lowrys buy some, seein' as how they've been shippin' hides. Nobody else that I'd know about except folks who like a bit on their vittles."

"You might keep it in mind and ask a few questions for me. I'd like to know." Then he got up abruptly and started for the door, leaving Hickey to look blank. "Now I've got to look in on Dolan. He ought to be sober enough to talk a bit by this time."

Dolan wasn't. He had been prolonging his spree by additional drinking, and Burdick remained only long enough to give the old man the care he needed. Then he went out again, more than a little sick at heart. Seeing a man go to seed like this was almost as bad as uncovering so much treachery among people he had once thought of as friends. It was going to be a relief to get away from Osage and its nastiness.

Immediately he was sorry for his mental indictment of the town. Osage was not so bad. Most of its people were pretty decent; it was just that the unexpected ones were turning out to be the villains. Partly to atone for his own unfair thoughts he returned to Hickey's office and took the willing lawman over to the Valley House for one of the enormous meals which Kennicott called lunch.

It gave them an opportunity to thresh out several matters, but Burdick refused to enlighten Hickey on the business of the salt. For one thing he was a little doubtful about its real importance and for a second reason he was enjoying the lawman's curiosity.

After that he stopped at the livery stable to get a bronc for the afternoon's trip to Fishel's, returning to his own quarters to find Ellen Davies already there.

"Finished so soon?" he inquired, surprised.

"So soon. There wasn't much to it. Stroud seems to be a most accurate record keeper. I might say that he always has been."

"Find anything?"

"Nothing out of the way. The stage line is still showing a small but steady profit. The freighting business is better, largely due to the hauling of sample ores from various prospect holes to smelter plants. Prospectors will pay the freight on several loads just to convince themselves that they haven't struck it as rich as they hoped they had."

"How many wagons?" he asked.

"Forty-two."

"All of them freighting ore?"

"Oh, no. About a dozen seem to be regularly employed in ordinary freight hauling, general supplies and the like. Others are doing the same sort of work around Butte, and a few are kept in reserve for emergencies. Actually I don't find very good records of but ten which are regularly used to haul ore. The others were listed as carrying miscellaneous loads. Mr. Stroud told me that it was mostly ore business."

"But their income was reported?"

"Yes."

"How much has Stroud been making out of the line lately? For himself, I mean."

"Last year the profit ran close to fifty thousand dollars. That was net. From that Stroud was paid his manager's salary of three thousand, leaving forty-seven thousand scant to be divided between him and your uncle."

"Then Stroud's quarter interest plus his salary must have brought him about fifteen thousand dollars."

"That's right."

"Got any idea what he's doing with it?"

"Only from gossip. The company's records naturally would not show it."

"Very well. What's the gossip?"

"He loses it as fast as he makes it, backing prospectors in hopes of striking something big like they did in Butte hill."

"Sounds likely. Then you don't think there's anything wrong with his books?"

"No. I don't think he would know how to make a smart job of falsifying books. I'm no real accountant, you know, but I think Stroud is a careful bookkeeper, not a clever one."

"Good enough estimate for me. What about the salt?"

She shook her head. "I wondered if you would ask about that. In the past three months there have been four barrels of salt brought in. Two went to Proctor's store, one to the Valley House, and one to Diamond K."

"Not very helpful," he commented. "Sounds normal enough." If she expected an explanation she was disappointed. Instead he asked, "Would the bank audit be too big a job for you to tackle this afternoon? I saw Whiteside this morning and told him you might be along. Don't do it if you feel it's too much."

"I'm on the payroll," she replied. "You're giving the orders."

"Take the bank chore, then," he said. "I've got to go have a look at Fishel."

"And Jane Lowry," she added. "Don't stay too long and get lost in the darkness like you did last night."

He covered his start of surprise. It was the first time she had ever attempted anything in the way of a pleasantry and he was not too sure that this try was good-humored. "Sure you're not worried about her being up there near that Bigelow lad?" he countered.

There was no mistaking the blush. "Forget that I said anything about it," she said hastily. "Jane Lowry means nothing to me—and neither does Dave Bigelow."

"That part," he said, his face perfectly straight, "I'm glad to hear."

Chapter Twelve

HE FOUND EVERYTHING QUIET at Fishel's cabin, but to his surprise it was Sadie Bigelow on duty. Miss Lowry was nowhere to be seen. "Afternoon, nurse," he greeted solemnly. "On duty ahead of time, aren't you?"

"Jes' come on. Miss Jane ain't more'n outa sight. She asked me to come over early today 'cause she wanted to do some of her own work at the ranch. I reckon she's mighty important over there."

The girl's tone indicated an abrupt change in her attitude toward Jane Lowry. Burdick led her on with: "Important, eh? I hadn't suspected. What does she do? Cook or shoe horses?"

The thin face puckered for a moment, then a smile broke through as Sadie recognized the attempt at humor. "Kinda had me guessin' there. I reckon we both been kinda wrong about Miss Jane. She's awful nice."

Burdick looked around at the spotless kitchen, remembering how it had looked as Fishel's eating-quarters. "Somebody sure did some work around here. Was that you or Miss Lowry?"

"She done most of it." Then she added slyly, "My pappy says Jane Lowry would shore make a danged good wife fer a doctor. She's got gumption enough to take care o' jest about everything while he keeps his mind on doctorin'."

Burdick grinned down at her. "Hey! Aren't you a little young for that kind of matchmaking talk?"

"Well, it's a good idea, ain't it? A doctor needs somebody to be nurse and tend house. Miss Jane could even keep his books; she does that at the spread. That's how come she went home today. Had to git a payroll ready."

"We'd better take a look at Fishel," Burdick said dryly.

The wounded man was still showing the effects of pain and shock, but his injuries were healing nicely. Moreover his attitude was cheerful and it didn't require many comments to determine that the cheerfulness was largely a by-product of Miss Lowry's nursing.

"Looks like we had the Lowrys all wrong, Doc," he said presently. "That gal jest cain't be no part o' the gang we been havin' trouble with."

Burdick changed the subject. He still remembered Jane Lowry's words about wanting those nester lands. She had not been entirely truthful then; maybe her present idea had its ulterior motive. Better to avoid comment until he knew a little more about that particular point.

"Did you ever happen to run across a short, stocky prospector named Noyes?" he asked abruptly. "I think they call him Loud Noyes. I don't know his real first name."

"Sure. I remember him. He stopped here mebbe three-four weeks ago. Said he was workin' fer yer uncle but wouldn't explain no more'n that."

"Which way was he headed?"

"Northwest. Kinda up the ridge."

"Toward Dog Robber Gulch?"

"I dunno the place. Ain't never done much meanderin' around. Too much work to be done right here in the bottoms."

"Think back. See if you can't date his visit a little more clearly."

Fishel was silent for some minutes, his frown of concentration a little theatrical. Finally he grunted unhappily. "Sorry. One day's a heap like any other to me. Best I kin tell ye is it musta been a little better'n a week before yer uncle got shot. I remember from goin' into Osage that Sattiday. I—"

"That's good enough. Exactly what I wanted to know. Now, is Miss Lowry planning to come back tomorrow?"

"She said she would."

"Good. Probably I'll be out to see you." Burdick watched the bearded lips draw into a sly grin. These folks had decided to like him and to like Jane Lowry. So they were promoting a bit of romance. The fact served his purpose well enough so he unblushingly used it. "In fact, I might even ride over to speak with her this afternoon. There's enough daylight left—and I ought to give her instructions for tomorrow."

He left to the accompaniment of several baldly encouraging remarks from Sadie Bigelow, heading upriver as though aiming for the Diamond K ranch house. Once out of sight of the Fishel cabin, however, he swung wide into a draw and worked his way around the southwest end of Hardtack Ridge. There he paused long enough to study the tracks which led into newly beaten trail to Dog Robber Gulch, then pushed on into a rocky defile which showed no trace of previous riders. So far as he could tell no one had passed through here since he had ridden the passage himself. Maybe no other person even knew of it. He had never told other folks much about his own exploring.

Presently he found himself in one of the narrow canyons which broke the apparently even slope of the divide. From the valley the mountain seemed almost smooth but Burdick knew that back here beyond Reveille Canyon there were many of these twisting, irregular passages, most of them little more than big cracks in the rocks as though the supports of the mountain chain had pulled away from the main group of peaks.

He rode swiftly northward for perhaps a half hour, following the canyons and coming eventually to a tangled mass of broken stone where the canyon formation ended in complete confusion. Down the slope to his right, he knew, would be the prospect holes of the Dog Robber Gulch and Reveille Canyon region while up the slope to his left was more of the broken country.

Today there was no smell of sulphur coming down from the heights and he could spot no telltale wisp of smoke. Still he scanned the ground carefully even as he took precautions against running into an ambush. Some two hundred yards across the rocky hollow he found what he had expected, a reasonably well defined trail up the ridge, a trail on which wagons had moved.

For a minute or so he was tempted to follow the sign but better judgment prevailed. Nothing could be gained by taking the risk and the afternoon was already drawing to a close. He had achieved his object in verifying the trail which he had reasoned would be here; better to get back to Osage and take the normal steps. After all he was trying to become a practicing physician, not a one-man Vigilante Association.

Again it was fully dark before he galloped into Osage, heading directly for the livery stable to leave the horse.

"Charge another one," he told Wilson. "At this rate it would be cheaper for me to buy a bronc."

"Mebbe not," Wilson retorted in his almost painful wheeze. "Yo'd have to have somebody to take care of the critter. Yo're a doctor now, not a wrangler."

"Right enough," Burdick agreed, remembering the pointed remarks of Sadie Bigelow. "Now that I'm supposed to keep my mind on medicine I'll need somebody to keep house, tend to my horse, act as nurse, and handle my accounts. At least that's what I was told this afternoon."

Wilson's grunt of surprise changed to a hoarse chuckle as Burdick added the final statement. "Sounds like some female woman's been tryin' to hook yo' into the blessed bonds o' matrimony."

"Not exactly. This was a promotion job, not an application."

"Huh? Oh, I see what yo' mean. Who was gittin' permoted? Sounds like it mighta been Ellen Davies. She comes about as close to answerin' the description as anybody I know."

"She does, doesn't she?" Burdick murmured. Then, as he turned away he added, "Oddly enough, Whispering, it wasn't Miss Davies that was being suggested—but it's an idea."

As he went out into the smooth darkness of early evening he was just in time to witness a flurry of action where a belated stagecoach was arriving at the stage line office. He started to stroll slowly in that direction, curious to see what new development had transpired, but as he drew nearer he saw a man running toward Hickey's office. Burdick crossed the street promptly, arriving simultaneously with the runner.

He did not know the man but the fellow's message brought him to instant attention. Dillingham had been picked up along the trail and was in bad shape.

"Git him over here!" Hickey barked. "Mebbe this is

where we git some information."

"Change that!" Burdick cut in. "Take him to my place. He'll need care as well as questioning. All right with you, Sheriff?"

"Take him to Burdick's," Hickey directed. "Make it fast."

By the time they had lighted lamps in the Burdick house two men were bringing a limp, battered figure. Dillingham certainly had the appearance of a man who had been through a rough time but he was still able to grin. Even two beautiful black eyes and a lot of lost skin hadn't killed his impudence.

"Seems like I finally arrived in the promised land, gents," he gasped. "Although you're the ugliest pair of angels I ever saw."

"When did you ever see an angel?" Burdick retorted. "And when do you think you ever will see one?" He was smiling in spite of his concern over the other's injuries.

"Don't ask questions," Dillingham sighed, almost falling into a chair. "Just patch me up so I won't leak at the seams."

Burdick went to work swiftly, assisted by one of the men who had helped Dillingham from the stage station. The other was Slats McGill, the stage driver, and Hickey got the story from him without delay.

"I kinda took him fer dead at fust," McGill declared, "but he shucked out of it right away. Musta slept all the way to Osage and he's lookin' better already." His broad wink was eloquent as he added, "A couple of snifters o' Valley Tan didn't hurt him none, I reckon."

"Where'd yuh pick him up?"

"Calamity Rock. I ain't shore how he got there; he ain't been what yuh might call real talkative. All I knowed was he was the jigger the bandits took the other day so I brung him in. Let me know how he gits along; I gotta take care o' the hosses."

The other man went along with him, a little reluctantly, and Hickey went over to watch while Burdick attended to the numerous abrasions on the peddler's body. "What happened to yuh, son?" the lawman inquired.

Dillingham was squinting with the pain but he managed to open one battered eye long enough to look from the sheriff to Doctor Burdick. Then he closed the eye again and said shortly, "I got beat up."

Burdick interpreted the glance. "This is Sheriff Hickey. He's the local law and he's a pretty good fellow. But don't talk to him unless you feel up to it. He'll wait."

"I could use a drink," Dillingham said, trying to grin. "I'm not working now so I'll indulge myself."

Hickey was frowning at the queer conversation, getting little help when Burdick explained, "Mr. Dillingham is a swindler by trade, Tex. He has to stay sober in order to outwit the suckers. Better give him a drink and protect our honest citizens."

"Hey! What's goin' on here?" Hickey rumbled.

"Anyway he's not working now," Burdick continued, still casual. "Get him a small snort."

Dillingham swallowed the liquor and seemed to brace up a little, telling his story with frequent interruptions as treatment of open wounds made him catch his breath.

"You know about the holdup, of course. Mebbe you didn't know that they grabbed me in mistake for you."

"We were pretty sure that was the way of it," Burdick told him, trying to save him the labor of relating known facts. "We've even got a pretty good idea why they wanted me. Go on from there."

"Shucks! I thought I'd surprise you with that part. Well, anyway, they prodded me along on that nag until I was saddle-sore all the way to my shoulder blades. I tried to ask 'em what they wanted but nobody would answer me. All I got was a gun muzzle in the back and an order to shut my big mouth."

"Score one for the bandits," Burdick said solemnly.

"Wait a bit," Hickey interrupted. "There was a halt right after they hit back from the trail. What happened there?"

Dillingham's astonishment was clear, and Burdick explained tersely, "The sheriff reads sign—when he looks in the right place and finds it."

"Kinda cute, eh? Yeah, we stopped but not for long. All they done was to tie that trunk on a hoss. The lad who was juggling it on the saddle horn in front of him was gettin' fed up with his act."

"That all, huh?" Hickey growled, disappointed.

"That was all. After that we rode like I told you. A long time after dark we stopped and they made camp. That was where they busted open the trunk. A couple of 'em helped themselves to things they wanted. Then they asked me, almost polite, if there was anything I wanted to take along with me. That was when I first got the idea they'd grabbed me in mistake for you.

"I told 'em I didn't want anything and right after that we started to ride again. That time we rode all right and I was half dead when we pulled in at another camp somewhere back in the mountains."

"How many men?" Hickey asked.

"Five."

"Can you describe any of them?"

"Sure. I had plenty of time to memorize every ugly phiz in the lot. Two were tall and lanky, looked like cowboys to me. One of 'em was redheaded and freckled, but the other was older and a mite bald. Also he had buck teeth."

"Red Worrell and Buck McGinness!" Hickey exclaimed. "I'll bet a hat!"

"That's what they called 'em," Dillingham agreed. "Red and Buck."

"Part-time Diamond K riders," Hickey growled.

Burdick did not comment, and Dillingham continued. "Then there was an old fellow with a foreign accent. Maybe Italian or Mexican; I can't tell the difference. Another was short and scrawny but with an awful big nose and squinty eyes. The leader was a big rascal, tough, ugly, and mean. All of 'em were a few days away from their last shaves but only the foreign one seemed to wear hair as a regular face decoration. He had a full beard, kinda shot with gray."

"I don't know none o' them others," Hickey mused. "Hear any names?"

"Only nicknames. I figgered they was bein' careful not to use anything else. The foreigner was Cooky, seein' as he did the honors. The little gent was Squint and the boss was Ramrod."

Again Hickey shook his head hopelessly, and Dillingham went on. "They kept me there all that day and the next night. Mostly I slept but once they tried to rout me out to fix up a place on the cook's hand where he'd burned himself. I tried to tell 'em I didn't know anything about it but they insisted I was a doctor. That's when I was sure they'd made a mistake—but it didn't do me a bit a good. All I got out of it was a beatin'. After they'd slugged me around a bit they went away and fixed up the cook's paw themselves.

"It was about noon o' the next day that a short, stocky ape busted in. I took it they'd been waitin' for him but right away he started to raise hell. Rawhided 'em somethin' fierce for grabbin' the wrong man."

"Did they call this fellow by name?" Burdick asked.

"No. Just called him Noisy."

Hickey let out a sort of smothered whoop, but Burdick merely asked, "Was he the man we fought with in Butte?"

"Say! That's a hunch! Of course, I wouldn't be able to tell. I never did see that gunnie in Butte. He was just a tough *hombre* with a lot of fists and elbows—and a hard head."

"But the voice. Could it have been the same?"

Dillingham's swollen eyes almost opened. "Doggone if you're not right. I knew I'd heard that growl before. And the build was right, too!"

"We're getting warm," Burdick commented. "Go on."

"Not much more to tell. For a while I thought they would hang me just for spite but instead they broke camp in a hurry and went away. I tried to talk 'em out of leavin' me but nobody paid me any mind. So, when they were out of sight, I started hoofing it back over what I thought was the way we'd gone in."

"Sounds like a tough hike to me," Hickey grunted.

"It was! I kept goin' until I tumbled over some kind of ledge in the dark. That's when I got the extra scrapes and digs. I slept right where I fell, just about used up. Next morning I slugged on again, tryin' to keep my directions straight. It was just getting dark again when I stumbled on what looked like a trail. The next I knew was when I opened my eyes and found myself bein' dumped into a stagecoach."

He slumped then, evidently having talked away the slight reserve of strength left to him after his ordeal. Burdick motioned to Hickey for assistance and they carried the maltreated one upstairs and put him to bed.

Back in the front-room office Hickey stared significantly at Burdick. "It all adds up," he growled. "Noyes showed up in the hills just in time to fit that yarn. Looks like the next move is to throw a loop around the varmint."

"Not yet. I want somebody else."

"Sure. You're after the ranny what killed yer uncle—but this Noyes is shore hooked up with him. If we grab Noyes we'll make him lead us to the big feller."

"Too much risk, Tex. We already know that the gang is a big one. Dillingham mentions six. Then there's the pair who jumped me at the Big Hole Saloon. The three who cut Fishel's wire are in it, too. Add the ringleaders and we've got quite an army to fight before we could even pick up Noyes. I don't propose to risk the lives of honest posse members against that kind of odds unless I'm mighty sure that we'll get the man we really want."

"But we gotta—"

"And another thing. Our real quarry has been smart. I can't tie him up with a thing except by some reasoning that's almost guessing. Perhaps he has confederates in town who are as clever as he is. If we let this leak out to them in getting our posse together we'll spill the beans."

"But we gotta do somethin'! This can't go on like it's goin'."

"Let me figure it tonight. We can't move until morning at best. Maybe I can hit on something."

Hickey still protested, but Burdick insisted. "I'm trusting you, Tex, even though my brain tells me I shouldn't trust anyone until I'm sure of a few more facts. Let me do it my way, will you? I think something's going to explode before long, something that will help us instead of the other side."

Chapter Thirteen

IT WAS A LONG EVENING for Doctor Frank Burdick. Twice he went upstairs to make sure that Dillingham was sleeping quietly but for the most part he divided his time between scanning records and trying to think of something he had missed. It was aggravating to know most of the answers and not be able to tie in the last vital link. Maybe he would simply have to wait for that expected explosion —which wasn't a very good prospect, no matter how optimistic he had sounded in mentioning it to Tex Hickey.

He had just blown out the lamp in the office when he caught the sound of running footsteps at a little distance. There was something light yet frantic about the patter which brought him to sudden alertness. He groped swiftly for the desk drawer, grabbing up the six-gun which he had cached there. Maybe it was old habit, maybe a sixth sense, but somehow he knew that he wanted a gun handy.

A couple of quick strides took him to the still-open front door, his eyes straining to adjust themselves to the darkness. Across the street the running feet were coming closer, distinct now on the hard-packed earth but blended with a heavier tread of pursuing footsteps. He made out a moving shadow, realizing that this was not just another brawl. Both running figures were keeping a tight silence. By that time the first one was crossing the street toward him, a distant flicker of lamplight providing enough illumination for him to realize that the fugitive was a woman. Instantly he knew that it was Ellen Davies. Not that he could actually see her; he simply knew it, never doubting his hunch.

"This way," he called softly as she reached the front yard. "What's up?"

There was no reply, only the gasps of the breathless girl as she fairly charged into him. By that time the pursuer was also crossing the street and this time the vagrant gleam of light glinted on metal. The man was carrying a gun in his hand!

Burdick had caught the girl in his arms but now he swung her behind him, shielding her even as he freed his gun hand. "Who is it?" he whispered, not turning his gaze away from the dark figure which was already directly in front of the door.

Her voice cracked from nervousness and want of breath as she gasped, "He—he's trying—to kill me." The last words went up to a high note which brought the pursuer to a halt. Burdick heard rather than saw the stop, for a split second thinking that the fellow was about to turn in retreat. The idea was promptly refuted. A roar of sound broke the flat hush, and the blackness of the night was split by two vicious streaks of orange flame.

Something stung Burdick's neck but he scarcely flinched. Black anger at the attack had blanketed every other thought in his mind, even the nervousness which he had felt without admitting it. He fired at the flashes, grimly, deliberately, knowing that his first slug had struck home but unwilling to have any mercy on the unknown thug. Only after he had squeezed the trigger three times did the black mood drop away, leaving him to the knowledge that the enemy was down, that he had started to fall at the first shot.

Somewhere at a great distance he heard his own voice saying, "Light the lamp, will you, Ellen? And look out for it; it's still hot." The sound seemed oddly impersonal, particularly the part about the hot lamp. It didn't sound at all like the voice of a man who had just killed someone, someone he didn't even know. Maybe this was all a bad dream in the first place.

Questioning yells from several near-by spots told him that it was no dream. Already swift shadows were closing in on the scene, Sheriff Hickey's demands louder than any of the others.

A light flared behind him as he jammed the gun back into his belt and went out to kneel beside the still figure on the sidewalk. A steady hand swept a match into flame and he grunted with astonishment to see the inert body of Dan Whiteside. The dapper little banker was quite dead, a wet spot showing in the center of the dark-blue shirt he had been wearing. At his side, still partly held in limp fingers, was a shiny thirty-eight revolver.

For the moment surprise left him speechless. He didn't know exactly what he had expected but certainly it had not been this. Whiteside had not entered into his calculations at all. He was still staring when men began to crowd around, asking the inevitable questions.

"Better get a lantern, somebody," he said, his voice weary. "You'll find one in the back of the house somewhere. Hickey, you'd better stay here. I don't want anybody to mess up the evidence."

"What evidence?" the panting lawman demanded.

Burdick waited until a man started through the house as directed, then replied, "The guns. Here's mine. You'll find three shots fired, I think. In Whiteside's gun there ought to be two empties. He fired twice and you'll find the marks of his bullets somewhere in or through the front doorway." Then he turned and went into the house, leaving the investigation to the sheriff. The feeling of being in the middle of a bad dream was coming back again and he didn't propose to talk too much while he felt that way. He wanted time to think, time to re-estimate the pattern of crime which he had so carefully puzzled out.

He exchanged glances with Ellen, neither of them

offering to speak. Then he dropped heavily into a chair. Almost without knowing it he heard the voices outside where Hickey was having trouble in following the regular routine. Doc Dolan, as coroner, was not able to appear, and Kennicott was assuming temporary authority in a sort of impromptu Mayor's Court.

Burdick didn't gather himself together until the proceedings were brought inside. Then he noted with something like normal interest the fussy display of self-importance on the part of Sam Kennicott. The stout man was evidently enjoying the role of judge but still he used skill in arranging matters. He took the seat behind the desk, his back to an inner wall. On his right Sheriff Hickey took up a belligerent position while Ellen and Burdick found themselves at his left. The four of them thus faced the crowd of townsmen who had jammed themselves through the front doors. One look at those tense faces indicated that a lot of folks wanted to know why a respected citizen like Dan Whiteside had been shot down.

Mayor Kennicott made a brief speech which Burdick took to be a warning to the crowd even though it sounded more like election campaign material. Then the fat man said abruptly, "Tell your story, Doctor Burdick."

Burdick told it, briefly and concisely, concluding, "I believe he fired at the sound of Miss Davies's voice. I didn't even know who he was at the time. I simply blazed away in self-defense."

"Did he hit either of you?" Hickey asked, looking oddly at Burdick.

"I'm all right," Ellen replied for herself, her voice still shaky.

Burdick put a hand to the side of his face, remembering that opening sting. His fingers encountered something sticky but no more. "I suppose his first slug tore a splinter out of the doorjamb. Something cut me a little—but it couldn't have been a bullet."

Nobody said a word for a long minute. They were listening intently and for the most part skeptically. None of them could quite picture Dan Whiteside as the type to go rushing around town in the darkness shooting at girls like Ellen Davies.

Finally Kennicott asked, "Why was Whiteside trying to shoot her?"

A burly man near the door laughed derisively. "Wrong question, Sam. How do we know he *was* chasin' her? Maybe she was here all the time and Whiteside found out about it."

Burdick stood up just as Bob Davies turned on the speaker. It was Sam Kennicott's bass that roared them both back to their places. "We'll have none o' that talk, Ives. Quiet, everybody! We'll let Ellen Davies speak for herself."

The crowd subsided, partly at the mayor's order and partly because Ellen had risen to her feet. Burdick could sense that she was fighting for self-control but he didn't think any of her other listeners realized it. She seemed quite sure of herself as she said, "I'd better tell it from the beginning, if you don't mind."

"By all means do," Kennicott agreed, lowering his voice once more and becoming the grave and reverend judge.

"This evening I was over at Holladays' with my parents. About eleven o'clock I decided to go home, my folks staying for another round of the card game they were playing. I met no one as I passed along the street but just as I turned in at our door I saw someone move in the shadows at the corner of Proctor's store. It made me a little nervous because the movement seemed so stealthy. I closed the door behind me and turned to look out. A man hurried along to turn in at the alley which runs between our place and Proctor's. I saw a glint of light on something and knew that he held a gun."

"Did yuh recognize the man?" It was Hickey asking the question.

"Not then."

"But yuh did later?"

"Yes. I slipped back into the kitchen and looked out

just in time to see him come around into the back yard. He tried the latch on the back door but it was fastened. Then he went around the other way, trying two windows on the far side. There was a little more light on that side and when he came close to a window I saw that it was Mr. Whiteside. I could also see the gun clearly.

"I guess I don't need to tell you I was afraid. I can only say I had more reason to be afraid than any of you know— and I can't tell you why."

"Better tell us," Kennicott urged. "It's important, you know."

"But I can't tell. Believe me, there was a reason, just as there is a reason why I can't explain. Anyway, the important thing is that he was out to kill me and I knew it. I waited until he had gone to the front of the house, then I made a deliberate noise in the kitchen. I could hear his footsteps as he came running toward the back so I tiptoed out through the front door and ran across here."

"Why?" It was Sheriff Hickey again.

"That's a part I can't explain. Just believe me that I had to find Doctor Burdick before Whiteside could catch up to me."

The audience reaction was not so good, Burdick decided. He could guess what Ellen was holding back but he didn't see why she was holding it. Her refusal was only adding to the dubious hostility of the onlookers.

"Go on with yore story," Kennicott said curtly.

"I ran as hard as I could, knowing that I'd fooled him for only a minute. I could hear him chasing me but he didn't gain much. I was more scared than ever when I saw that this house was dark but fortunately for me Doctor Burdick was here and the door was open. After that everything happened just as Doctor Burdick has already described it."

She slumped back against Burdick, the tension getting her almost before she uttered her final statement. The crowd muttered ominously, hesitating to believe this fanciful story of a Dan Whiteside who had run amuck. Once he might have been a sturdy sort of character, back in the freighting days, but of late years he had been a quiet man, keeping to himself and indicating his interest in the world only by his vanity. It was hard to think of Whiteside in the role Ellen Davies had described.

Under cover of the mutters Burdick whispered in the girl's ear. "They don't believe you. Better tell them the rest."

"But I can't. It's the bank. They'll mob the place if they hear Whiteside has been stealing from it."

He was not overly surprised. No other answer had seemed possible. "It'll be worse if they don't know. Tell them."

She shook her head as Kennicott banged a gun butt for order. "Anybody got anything else?" he roared.

Burdick stood up again, speaking swiftly but calmly. "Quite a little, Mayor. It's fairly obvious that these folks are having trouble believing that Dan Whiteside was a murderous midnight prowler. I can't blame them but I think they'll understand when they learn why he was driven to desperation."

He shook off Ellen's restraining hand, talking to the audience rather than to the lawmen as he explained, "Today I asked Miss Davies to audit the bank's books, a part of the routine in settling my late uncle's estate. She found something incriminating to Whiteside but was unable to report to me this evening because I returned late and was immediately kept busy by another matter. Whiteside evidently realized that she had learned something damaging to him. I think he must have been ready to give up but then he found out that Miss Davies had not been able to get to me with her report. So he decided to silence her before she could."

He caught the new note of belief in the murmur which greeted the words, hastening to clinch it by adding, "I think you'll understand why she was unwilling to tell this story. Banks have been ruined by less serious rumors. Miss Davies was willing to let you think ill of her rather than to be the cause of any sort of run on the local bank."

Kennicott rumbled uneasily, "How'd yo' know this if Ellen didn't have a chance to tell yo' about it?" He was forgetting his dignity a little and letting the words slur.

Burdick smiled. "She just whispered enough so I could guess the rest. However, now that I've talked this much she can feel free to tell you the whole story. I think it will be better that way."

She shook her head wearily. "There isn't much more to tell. This afternoon I found that the bank's books had been clumsily altered. I'm no bank examiner but any casual bookkeeper could have spotted it. I tried to pretend I wasn't seeing anything out of the way but a couple of my early questions must have tipped Mr. Whiteside off to what I was thinking. When I stopped asking him about the false entries he must have realized why I didn't talk any more."

"Better tell these folks what kind of account-juggling had been going on," Burdick suggested, aware that a new note of tension had come into the room. Most of these people were depositors and they were beginning to worry about the safety of their money.

"Actually it wasn't on a very large scale," Ellen said quietly, as though aware of the tension. "Whiteside seemed to have borrowed several small sums from the safe, probably for personal speculations. In some instances he must have replaced the money but of late he had not been covering up with any replacements."

"How much is the bank short?" Burdick asked, phrasing the question which he knew was in the mind of every listener. Better to get it over.

"I'm not expert enough to answer that. I didn't have time or opportunity for any sort of thorough audit, you know. Maybe I'm not even a good enough accountant to do the chore."

"Make a guess. It's pretty important to all of us."

"Very well. It's a guess. I think the shortage is well under ten thousand dollars. The bank is still perfectly sound."

"If folks don't git panicky and try to haul out their dinero," Hickey growled.

Again there was that uneasy murmur from the crowd but this time it was on a note which boded no personal ill for Doctor Burdick. They weren't much concerned with the killing now; they were simply worried depositors in a bank whose manager had been detected stealing.

Suddenly Kennicott banged the gun butt down on the desk again, demanding order in his most stentorian tones. His very manner proclaimed that he was about to make a speech, and the crowd's mutter subsided a little. Sam Kennicott's speeches were likely to be almost anything. Even jittery depositors could wait to hear what he had to say. This time Sam didn't disappoint anybody.

"Gents," he boomed, "I reckon we've come up with some mighty important answers tonight. I figger we now know how our friend Jefferson Burdick was killed."

That did it. Men forgot money worries to listen. Kennicott waited for the hush which followed the first gasp of surprise, continuing, "It ain't hard to see why Dan Whiteside thought he could kill Ellen to stop her tongue. He'd already got away with it once—and in this very room. It stands to reason that he killed Jeff Burdick for the same exact purpose that he tried to kill Ellen—because Jeff had found out about the bank monkeyshines."

There was a prompt uproar, and Kennicott smiled with satisfaction. Burdick tried to make himself heard but was unable to do so. Finally it was the fat man who managed to get order once more. "This here's a court," he yelled. "Don't forget it! We got a decision to make and I'm appointin' yo' all jurymen. What do yo' find in the charge against Frank Burdick?"

There was a reflection of the old Vigilante days in the prompt chorus of the "jury." Men who had been openly suspicious only minutes before shouted, "Not guilty!" in unison, then crowded to shake Doctor Burdick's hand. By that time he had decided to keep his protest to himself.

Better to let matters go as they were going.

It took nearly an hour to get rid of the crowd, but finally no one was left in the room but Burdick, Hickey, Ellen Davies, and her father. Kennicott had been politician enough to head for the nearest saloon with his enthusiastic constituents.

It was then that Dillingham put in his appearance. He had thrust his legs into a pair of Burdick's trousers and the nightshirt bulging above the waistline put the extra touch of comedy to his battered appearance. "Nice show," he observed briskly. "Too bad I didn't have anything to sell while that fat gent was pourin' on the oil. It woulda been a pipe!"

"Go back to bed," Burdick ordered.

"Not on your life! I think you're in a bad spot, brother, so I'm taking cards in the game. Maybe I can pull something off the bottom of the deck."

"Meaning what?" Burdick snapped.

"The bank, my friend. I take it you're a new hand in the banking business, however you managed to get into it so doggone fast. Maybe you don't know the trick rules of the game. A bank has to stay open regular times and they've got to be able to meet all depositors' demands in those hours. If they don't—they shut up shop and fight it out with the law. Usually it means they go broke—if they ain't busted already."

"But this bank is sound. Miss Davies just said so."

"Sound—but not solvent." He grinned. "I know all the words, you see. That comes from associating with big men in the banking graft and other associated criminal classes."

"What's this jasper up to?" Hickey growled.

Dillingham winked as broadly as a swollen eye would permit. "Don't throw your fleas on me, lawdog. I'm on the up-and-up this time. I'm telling you there ain't one bank in a thousand can stand a run. If they've got cash enough on hand to meet a sudden rush of their depositors they ain't makin' money. If they're doin' a sound business their cash is tied up in loans that'll bring a profit. This local interest factory may have plenty of assets but it won't have the hard cash to handle the demands. Come daylight a flock o' nervous citizens are goin' to waltz right in and allow as how they've had enough bankin' business for the immediate present."

"He's quite correct," Ellen said, almost in a whisper. "Give the bank time to call in loans and every depositor could be paid. If a run starts tomorrow the place will have to close. Then anything can happen. At the very best the town will be without banking service almost indefinitely."

"And with a dozen payrolls due tomorrow," Hickey added. "It ain't good."

Burdick asked thoughtfully, "Are you sure the amount missing is no more than you stated, Ellen? It seems pretty small to make a man commit murder."

"I told you I was guessing," she retorted. "But I'll give odds the bank isn't hurt."

Hickey pulled at his whiskers. "Ten thousand dollars didn't make up the whole story for Whiteside. Discovery meant ruin, regardless of how many dollars it added up to."

"And it means ruin for the bank if we can't find a way to kill off a possible run."

Bob Davies spoke for the first time in long minutes, his frown deepening as he addressed his daughter. "Ellen, I think you'd better come along home with me. Folks will be talking already. You can't spend the rest of the night riskin' both your life and your reputation."

"That's right," Burdick agreed. "I'm sorry your daughter had to get into this at all. I'm mighty thankful for what she has done and I'll certainly see that she is paid— but she'd better get out now."

Ellen Davies stared at him with something like the old tomboy grin quirking at the corners of her mouth. "Don't count me out yet—either of you," she retorted. "I picked this kind of work because I felt I could handle it. I don't propose to run for cover just because the job has stopped being easy. You go home, Father; I'm staying to see this through."

Argument was useless. They tried, but the girl had her mind made up, a source of some satisfaction to Burdick. He appreciated the loyalty and he knew that he needed her. She knew more about the bank than any living person.

With that in mind he said finally, "Have it your way—and thanks again. Now tell us what we'd better do first."

Again the fleeting grin appeared, but her words were serious and thoughtful. "I think you'd better send a messenger to Butte with a hurry call for cash help. W. A. Clark's bank was always friendly to your uncle. Ask them for all the cash you can put up security for. Have it rushed here and we'll try to stall the depositors with the cash on hand until the help arrives."

"Sounds smart," Dillingham cut in. "And I'll offer another idea. It's gradually been seepin' into my fuzzy brain that you're a right opulent sort of citizen. You seem to own a few prosperous hunks of property in this vale of fat cows and raw money. Right?"

"Probably," Burdick agreed. "I don't exactly know how much."

"But you could put up enough to get that extra cash?"

"Of course." It was Ellen answering the question.

"Then the problem is time. And I've got a hunch you oughta be able to lay your hands on a sizable poke of the shiny tin. Every stage line I ever got near seemed to handle their own cash in nice, generous chunks."

"That's it!" Ellen exclaimed. "Stroud always kept quite a bit of cash in the office. Lots of people think of an express business as a sort of bank out in this country."

"Then I got an idea," Dillingham announced. "We send for extra cash. Then we tell the good citizens that the bank is temporarily out of business because Whiteside died without tellin' anybody where he hid the keys. But we'll be open-souled public benefactors and keep the wheels of commerce and industry in their dear old ruts by tidin' folks over with funds out of the stage company's safe. It oughta make a good impression and keep anybody from squawkin' till the big money arrives. Smart, eh?"

"No," Burdick said decisively.

"No? Why not?"

"Because I don't propose to start fooling people. This thing has to be played out with all cards on the table."

Both Ellen and Hickey started to remonstrate but Dillingham took over once more, forcing his way into the lead through sheer impudence. "Gosh! Sometimes it's awful monotonous to be honest. Then let's go have a peek at the quarters of the late unlamented. Maybe the polecat *did* hide his keys. That'd help."

"You men do the looking," Ellen said quietly. "I'm going to Butte. And don't argue with me. I'll get action there and I don't think any of the rest of you can. They know me."

Hickey moved suddenly. "That makes sense. Come on, Ellen. We'll rout Whisperin' outa his haypile and send him in with yuh. Git outa town as quiet as yuh kin. I'll be back here in a jiffy and the rest of us kin make a search o' Whiteside's room."

Burdick felt a sense of annoyance at having the play thus taken away from him but he couldn't find any good objection to any of the proposals. The whole thing was a mess, whichever way he looked at it. Only hours before he had been trying to think up a good way to close out the whole story of trouble—and now he was into something he didn't even begin to understand.

Chapter Fourteen

DAWN WAS BREAKING before the proposed plans could be carried out. There was some delay in getting the messengers out of town; Bob Davies objecting quite strenuously to his daughter's activities while Whispering Wilson was more than a little reluctant to undertake the mission. Hickey and the girl carried the point, however, and the pair slipped away apparently without attracting attention.

The search of Whiteside's room had also taken a lot of time, the results being good or bad depending upon the viewpoint. Burdick was disturbed at not finding either bank keys or any record of a safe combination but Dillingham was frankly elated. His plan could now be carried into effect and it was clear that he intended to handle the operation himself.

"My chore," he told Burdick, his battered features twisted into a sort of embarrassed grin. "Of course it sounds like a big risk to put a bad character like me on a money job—sorta in a class with sendin' a rabbit to bring home lettuce—but you're stuck, chum. This chore needs a lad with a gift of gab and I'm just the gabby individual you require. Maybe it'll do me good to be running an honest graft for a change."

Burdick chuckled. "You're hired," he agreed. "I'll go along with you while we bulldog Virgil Stroud into producing the cash but after that you're on your own."

"Not quite," Hickey interrupted. "I ain't jest shore what this pilgrim is up to. I'm goin' to be watchin' him right sharp."

"I'll even like that," Dillingham agreed. "It'll be the first time I ever had a lawman watching my pitch when he wasn't conspirin' with himself to restrain trade."

By the time they had their plans laid the town was astir. Question-Mark Turpin turned up early at the Burdick place, his round little face excited but at the same time almost mournful. "Plenty stirred up out there," he greeted. "And I had to miss all the fun. First time in months I've been to bed at a respectable hour, too! Oughta be a lesson to me. How are you givin' out the facts?"

Burdick studied the frowsy little man with some caution. Turpin had seemed genuinely friendly from the first but somehow he hadn't been too successful in his avowed intention of swinging public opinion behind Burdick. No issue of the local paper had appeared yet but there was nothing to indicate that the man had convinced anyone with oral efforts. Maybe he was really a friend and maybe he wasn't.

"I guess everybody knows the yarn," Burdick told him. "They stuck around here long enough." He talked swiftly, watching the erratic course of Turpin's stub pencil as the man took it all down. The little editor interrupted with a question or two when the explanation for Whiteside's attack was given, finally asking, "What steps are you taking, Frank? It'll only take a couple of loudmouth nuisances on the street and you'll have a full-sized run on the bank. I've seen it happen with less excuse."

Burdick answered tersely, telling the story they had decided should be given out. "The bank and the safe are locked. A search of Whiteside's room reveals neither a key nor a safe combination. We've sent to Butte for help. The bank itself seems to be completely solvent so until that help arrives we'll do emergency banking through the stage line company."

"You mean you've sent for somebody to bust open the safe?"

"I hope we don't have to burst it." Burdick smiled. "Butte ought to have some kind of locksmith in town, legal or otherwise."

Turpin laughed and didn't seem to notice that Burdick had not actually answered his question. It was a point which had been bothering the doctor for some time. Once he had suggested sending another messenger after Ellen with word to bring a safe expert but Dillingham had persuaded him against it, arguing that the girl would be smart enough to figure on something of the sort. She had not known about the missing key when she left Osage but would probably suspect that the combination was recorded only in Whiteside's memory.

"How much do you think Whiteside got away with?" Turpin was asking.

Burdick forced his thoughts back to the immediate subject. "Not very much, we believe. Miss Davies tells me that the bank's undivided profits will easily cover the shortage.

Apparently Whiteside was frantic at being found out, not at the actual amount of money he was short. Depositors will not be affected at all, even if I have to throw every dollar's worth of the estate's property into the pot."

"Better spread that word," Turpin suggested. "It might help."

"Start spreading," Burdick told him. "Get out a circular and send me the bill. Tell the story, completely and correctly. Then warn folks not to expect any miracles from the temporary bank at the stage line office. We've got some cash there and we'll try to spread it around where it'll do business the most good. I understand there are several small local payrolls to be met. We'll provide the cash so that men won't be cramped for money to live on. Our own payroll and Lowry's we'll try to handle on a proportion basis. If folks will co-operate we'll try to keep the town running financially until we can pry the bank open."

Turpin was scribbling furiously. "Anything else?"

"Yes. I want to see a proof on that before you print it."

The round face clouded but there seemed to be nothing but honest hurt in it. Burdick grinned, taking away any sting by adding, "Maybe I didn't put it as smart as I might have. Things don't look the same in print sometimes. Now get started, will you? The sooner folks see this in print the better we'll be."

The newspaperman hurried away, and Burdick had a few minutes in which to collect his harried thoughts. The collection was not pleasant. Ever since that night in Butte he had been under a strain, knowing that something was seriously wrong and never being able to put a finger on the trouble. Always there had been the threat of physical danger in the air, always that indefinable sense of being menaced—and never had he had the dubious satisfaction of knowing the true source of that menace. A man couldn't go on fighting shadows forever.

In the past day or two, of course, he had managed to spot some of the enemy's hired guns, but the rest of the problem was almost as dark as it had been from the very beginning. It was like knowing that the patient had a high temperature without being able to get the least inkling as to what was the cause of the fever. A case of sparring for time, treating the symptoms and hoping that the real virus would disclose itself before it could prove fatal.

And now there had been a turn for the worse. Complications had set in. The Whiteside shooting had thrust a whole new set of facts into the case, none of them fitting with the previously discovered information. Still thinking in medical terms he decided that it was like treating a mysterious and particularly malignant fever only to have the patient develop smallpox—and with no vaccine in the county!

He knew that he had blundered badly on the bank matter and wished he had been able to keep Ellen Davies in Osage. She was the brain of the company where such business details were involved but there had been no choice. She was also the only one who could have handled the Butte errand. It made him realize how completely he had come to depend upon her in the few days they had been working together. He could almost forget the way she had scorned him.

Maybe she still did. He knew that his claim upon her respect was pretty thin, almost solely a result of their joint efforts on behalf of Ned Fishel. Yet she had run to him for help when Whiteside began to stalk her. Had that been simply a businesslike matter of getting her story told or had she really wanted to come? He remembered the touch of her body as he had swung her through the doorway. It had been a brief contact, almost a frantic one, but he seemed to remember that there had been something more to it than a gesture of actual assistance. Maybe he was dreaming things—but the dream helped.

Dillingham came downstairs then, wearing Burdick's clothes with a jauntiness that even two black eyes could not discount.

"There is a mutter of discontent among the citizenry

on yonder village green," he announced, the flippancy not quite concealing a note of real concern. "Perhaps we had better pass benevolently among the peasants and give them the reassurance of our presence and a smooth spiel."

Burdick smiled fleetingly. "Don't overdo it," he warned. "We've got to persuade them, not entertain them."

"Trust me, chum. Maybe I'll even get them to sympathize with me when they see this lovely pair of shiners I'm wearing. Where's that bewhiskered brush-ape of a sheriff?"

"He's coming across the street now. Better mind your manners."

Dillingham tried to wink but it turned into a grimace of pain as he contorted the damaged eye. Again Burdick thought about the shakiness of his own position. In a crisis like the present one he was having to depend pretty heavily on a man whose reputation was something less than good. Dillingham wasn't even honest, let alone diplomatic.

Still, he stuck to the program they had already discussed. Hickey had already posted Deputy Moon Peckham at the bank with orders to tell the story as it would appear in Turpin's circular. The other three would proceed to the stage line office and set up shop there while Bob Davies had been asked to help Turpin. If nothing went wrong they might lull the fears of the depositors until cash could be brought in. Burdick didn't let himself even consider the fact that the Butte bankers might refuse to help.

They took plenty of time in walking down to the stage office. Not only were they anxious to put on a good show of leisurely confidence but it seemed like a good idea to stop and talk with the various people who asked questions. Regardless of phrasing, Dillingham's idea had been sound. The way to beget confidence was to talk with people and make them feel easy. Oddly enough, it was Sheriff Hickey who seemed to be getting the best results with his grumbling.

"That danged Doc Burdick's a plumb fool," he would

tell friends. "With all he's got on his mind he ain't got a speck o' business fussin' with this bank chore. But a feller can't reason with him. He wants folks to git dinero if they need it so I ain't arguin'. It's his money."

Burdick was feeling better when they reached the stage office but the relief came to an abrupt ending. The place was closed and locked.

A hostler came around from the stables, meeting Hickey's question with a shake of his grizzled head. "Stroud? Nope. He ain't been around since the mornin' stage shoved off for Butte. He got a saddle bronc outa the stable but I didn't see which way he went."

"With the cash, no doubt," Dillingham murmured. "Now we're in a mess."

It seemed like the logical explanation. Virgil Stroud had seen enough to know that the conspiracy was about to be exposed so he had salvaged what he could, getting out of town with the cash which had been kept in the company safe.

Hickey seemed to see it that way, his heavy voice rising to a pitch of harsh anger as he fired questions at the hostler. People were beginning to drift toward them, and Burdick intervened. "Easy, Tex. Try to keep matters as quiet as possible but find out which way Stroud went. Get moving!"

He waited until the lawman had drawn out of earshot, then he spoke swiftly to the softly cursing Dillingham. "Can you open a safe?"

The injured eyes were sharp and wary as the other man looked up. "I've seen it done," he replied guardedly. "It's not my graft but I reckon I could manage with a little luck and an old-fashioned box."

"Then come on. Uncle Jeff didn't seem to own but two keys, both tagged. One was for the house and the other was for this office. I've got it in my pocket."

They went in quickly, locking the door behind them and leaving the shades drawn. The people on the streets were going to do some fast thinking but it couldn't be helped. With only one chance available they had to take that one.

Dillingham went directly to the cumbersome iron safe behind the barrier, commenting, "It's locked. I didn't expect it would be. Seems like the jigger wouldn't bother to lock it after he eloped with the plunder."

"That's the point," Burdick said shortly. "I don't think he did rob the place. Stroud stands to gain more by sticking it out than he would by running. See if you can get that thing open."

Dillingham was already bending close, moving the dial gently and listening for the fall of the clumsy tumblers. "Write down these numbers," he directed presently. "We'll work it out, I think."

It took some time, Dillingham apologizing for his own errors with the repeated assertion that this was not his regular graft, but eventually he grunted with satisfaction, called a final number, and swung the door open.

"Shiny tin!" he breathed. "And green goods! A lot of it. Looks like you had this Stroud monkey figured right, after all."

"I've got to be right once in a while," Burdick told him with a rueful grin. "Stroud's a partner in this line. He's been up to some crooked work but I don't think he's in the big stink. Anyway, I can't prove it on him. It seemed like he'd try to play for the safe stakes."

"Got those numbers?" Dillingham interrupted.

"Sure."

"Let me look." He took the paper, picked up a pencil from Stroud's desk, and stared around him thoughtfully for a moment or two. Then he crossed to a back corner and lifted a brightly lithographed calendar which advertised Posthumous Pain Pills. "More fake remedies!" he exclaimed. "How do those quacks stay out of jail?" Then he carefully copied the safe combination on the wall and permitted the calendar to drop back into place.

Burdick was grinning again but he asked, "Can't you trust yourself to remember it—or were you planning to come back later?"

"You hurt my tender sensibilities, chum. And after I'd just showed my interest in reform by condemning Doc Sellers, too! No, partner, I'm using the old Dillingham brain. Have you considered what thoughts would pop into the skulls of the local worriers if they suspected their temporary bank was being operated by a gent who'd got hold of the petty cash by fiddlin' with the safe combination? The whole show would go bust. Now we'll show 'em the figures on the wall and tell 'em how lucky it was that Stroud had such a bad memory that he had to write notes like that. By the way, I didn't chalk up the right figures, in case somebody gets midnight ideas. Here's the paper."

Burdick shook his head. "I give up. Why did a man with your brains ever get into petty confidence games?"

"I never had a decent crack at anything else," he replied candidly. "But just watch my smoke on this stretch of track. When do we open our doors to the avid customers?"

"Might as well take the plunge right away. No, wait a minute. Hickey's coming back. We'll see what he's got to say first."

The sheriff didn't have much to report. Virgil Stroud had ridden away toward the northern mountains immediately after the departure of the morning stage. No one seemed to know any more than that. He hadn't spoken to anyone except the hostler at the company stable.

They tried their story on Tex and he took it without a blink, merely commenting on the luck involved. Then they opened the doors and waited for the trouble to start.

Out on the street they could see men talking together in small groups, eyes turning toward the stage station with increasing frequency. Presently a big fellow in Levi's and a loose flannel shirt strode purposefully toward the little office, entering with just a trace of bravado.

"They tell me a man can get a check cashed here," he blurted. "What about it?"

"Anything within reason—if it's a good check," Dillingham told him. "Got an account in the local bank?"

"Dang right I have. Close to five hundred on drawin' account. I want a hundred of it."

Dillingham looked at Hickey, and the lawman nodded. "This here's Mort Tew. I ain't in a spot to know his business or the bank's but he's an honest *hombre* and knowed to have a bank account. I reckon the check's plenty good."

"That's enough for us," Dillingham rejoined. "How do you want it, Mort?"

Other experimenters followed Tew, but there was no rush or disorder. Within the hour Dillingham cashed ten local bank checks and a small draft on the Miners Bank of Butte. He also refused to do business with two hopeful bums, Hickey turning thumbs down on their claims.

"Looks like they're convinced," Tex said hopefully after booting the second panhandler into the street. "And that's a plumb good sign. Mebbe folks are gettin' rid o' the mean ideas they been holdin' about yuh, Doc."

"I hope so," Burdick told him. "Regardless of other factors I'm getting tired of having half the people in town look at me as though they expected me to spit fire and brimstone."

Hickey let out a grunt of alarm and pointed up the street. A half-grown boy was running toward the stage office, tense emotion clear on the freckled face. "Now what?" Tex growled.

The answer came speedily enough. Quite out of breath the boy burst into the office, jerking a dirty thumb over his shoulder even before he could manage to gasp, "Doc Dolan! I think—I think he's dead!"

Burdick started for the door. "Hold the fort, gents," he said grimly.

He hurried up the street, taking the proof sheet which Question-Mark Turpin hurried out to thrust at him. He scanned it as he walked, handing it back with a terse: "Print it. Get it on the street as soon as you can."

Then he lengthened his stride a little, vaguely conscious that this new development might help to create a diversion and relieve the banking tension. For the most part, however, he was resentful. Dolan's death was not unexpected but it had come at a most inconvenient time, simply adding more smoke to the already troubled atmosphere. That had been the trouble with this whole show; so many things happened at the wrong time that a man never had a chance to put his mind on any one problem.

Doc Dolan was dead, no question about it. Burdick examined the old man's body with due care while curious onlookers crowded the doorway. Then he stared bleakly at the empty bottles which had appeared on the floor since his last visit. It was all pretty clear. Dolan had prolonged his spree, perhaps deliberately, until his tired old heart could no longer stand the gaff. Burdick calculated the total consumption of brandy and wondered how Dolan had ever been able to control himself enough to drink the last of it. Finally he turned to look into the eyes of the nearest men.

"Heart failure," he said quietly.

"With all them bottles?" a squatty little man exclaimed. "I'll bet he—"

"Heart failure, I said!" Burdick snapped. "Doc Dolan was a mighty good friend to me. I think he must have been to most of you. So it was heart failure."

He waited for someone to argue the point, eyes boring into them until the men in front edged back against their fellows. Finally a voice muttered, "Poor Doc. Tough that he had to go like that. He was a mighty fine doctor."

Burdick wondered. Dolan had been ignorant. He had blundered on cases where his mistake could never be proven against him. He might have killed Jefferson Burdick if a gunman hadn't stepped in first. Yet Dolan had handled a hard job in a hard country. He'd been a friend to people who needed him. He had fought through blizzards and summer heat to do his best for those in trouble. Maybe that was all that counted.

"That's right," Burdick said softly. "He was a mighty fine doctor. I hope I can do half as well."

Chapter Fifteen

IT WAS WELL PAST NOON before Burdick felt free to leave Dolan's place. Not that there was anything he could do for Dolan. It was simply that he was caught up in a whirl of public emotion from which he was unable to escape. People were suddenly realizing how much Doc had meant to most of them and a platoon of volunteers swarmed upon the house, every individual trying to do something just a little extra in memory of the departed. Burdick took proper precautions, locking away drugs, instruments, and records before turning the place over to the folks who were preparing for the funeral. In a way it was a satisfying sight. After several days of seeing Osage people as a sullen, suspicious lot it was a nice change to see them doing a thing like this.

Leaving the scene of brisk but sorrowful action he went back to his own quarters, hoping for a few minutes of privacy that would permit some thinking. His mind had scarcely touched on the Reveille Canyon problem since last evening even though he recognized that as being the big puzzle to be answered. Tex Hickey should have been turned loose on that business today if there were to be any hopes of real action. Instead the lawman was playing banker with a confidence man as partner. The funny angles in this case were no funnier than the strange combinations it was producing.

It was nearly three o'clock when Burdick gave up in disgust. His thoughts simply refused to obey orders. Maybe that was partly a matter of having so many things to think about; maybe it was simply weariness and loss of sleep. At any rate he was finding that logical reasoning came hard. Every time he tried to work out a reasonable relationship between Uncle Jeff's death and the smoke on the mountain he found himself wondering whether Ellen had reached Butte yet. Or would she get the cash? Or did Ned Fishel need attention today?

When he found himself brooding over the deaths of Whiteside and Doc Dolan he left the house irritably and started for the stage station. It was time to close the stop-gap bank, anyway. Folks had been convinced and were playing the game. No point in reaching out for trouble.

He found his bankers involved in a quiet game of crib-bage, apparently on the best of terms with each other. He smiled quietly, told them about the final arrangements for Dolan's funeral, and asked, "Anything important been happening?"

"Kinda slow after the novelty wore off," Dillingham said. "We had just one call for a sizable wad of cash. Money for the Diamond K payroll." He chuckled quizzically. "Kind of a surprise for me to find that the payroll boss was the same lady I buzzed so hard on the stagecoach the other day. I didn't figure she was in the blue chips like that."

Hickey cut in before Burdick could ask a question. "Jane and Rusty Aiken rode in for the payroll, Frank. They settled fer half and didn't make no fuss when we told 'em the bank'd likely be open in another day or so. The gal was goin' to stop over at yuhr place and tell yuh not to bother ridin' out to Fishel's today, seein' as he's doin' fine, but I knowed yuh was busy about then so I promised I'd pass the word."

"Partly my idea," Dillingham announced. "I didn't want her seein' too much of you while I'm so handicapped by these assorted discounts to my manly beauty. You got too many advantages now."

Burdick stared, trying to guess how serious the man might be. "Sounds like the same sales talk I got up the river." He grinned. "What's everybody trying to do, get me into a fight with Rusty Aiken?"

"Jane says she'll be nursin' again tomorrow," Hickey interrupted. "The Bigelow gal doubled up today so Jane could handle payroll. I was to tell yuh."

"Thanks. Now let's close up shop."

"Ready," Dillingham agreed. "I've kept a running record all day."

"Good. Any reserve left for tomorrow?"

"Some. It won't go far, though, if the stage line's payroll comes out. I was lookin' at Stroud's figures."

"We'll work it somehow. Ellen and Whisper ought to be back by late afternoon tomorrow—if they get the money. I figure they're in Butte now. If Ellen can talk to the right parties today she'll be ready to start back early tomorrow morning. If anything goes wrong—" He did not need to finish the sentence. Both of his hearers knew how thin was the ground under them. Folks were calm now but it didn't take much to excite worried bank depositors.

They were almost ready to leave the building when Virgil Stroud rode into the lane, both his horse and his person showing the clear effects of a lot of riding. He dismounted stiffly, looping the reins about a section of fence, and stalked in, several emotions fighting for predominance on his red face.

"What's all this?" he demanded. "Who let yo' in?"

"I have a key," Burdick told him. "When we learned that there was no way to get the bank open we decided to use the stage company's cash to tide folks over. It's hard on a town to get cramped without notice."

Stroud seemed genuinely distressed. "I never thought o' that," he confessed. "Too bad I had to make that trip today. We coulda put ourselves in right solid with folks."

"Maybe we did. Anyway, we went through with the idea."

"You what? But the safe—"

"We outguessed you," Dillingham interrupted. "Lots o' folks won't trust their own memories with safe combinations so they write the numbers down where they can find 'em easy. We figured you mighta done that so we scouted around till we found 'em."

"But I never— Say! That's right! I never rubbed those

numbers out after I wrote 'em there four years ago." He went around behind the barrier and stooped to squint upward at the under surface of the planking. "Still here, all right," he muttered. "Dam' smart of yo' to look for it."

"All in the day's work," Dillingham commented, winking at the astounded Burdick. The battered one didn't seem in the least surprised, and Burdick decided that it wouldn't have made any difference to him, anyway. He probably could have convinced Stroud that the figures behind the calendar had been similarly forgotten.

But they were the wrong numbers on the wall. How had he planned to— Burdick decided not to worry about it. Dillingham was finding all the answers; let him go on doing it.

"You'll find the accounts in order, Virgil," he said, switching the topic abruptly. "Try to hedge on your payroll tomorrow or tonight, whenever you're figuring the pay. We may have to get along without help for another day or so."

Stroud nodded, still apparently taking it all in stride. Burdick had expected some kind of protest but the stage line manager was stringing along as though in complete sympathy with the deal. "We'll work it out," he said.

Burdick tried another angle. "Out drumming up business today?"

"Not exactly. Part of the payroll job. We've been doing quite a bit of hauling this last couple of weeks for a funny mine outfit back in the hills. It was completely confidential. These two hardrock boys didn't know just what they'd struck so they wanted to get test ores shipped to Butte on the quiet before they let anybody know what they were up to. I let 'em have six wagons with crews. The men are sworn to secrecy and they don't come into Osage. I rode out to pay 'em today." He glanced at the others. "This is off the record, remember. We have to take care of customers."

Burdick nodded, the old sense of bafflement hitting him again. Stroud was being frank, telling a story which had a ring of truth in it. Then what—

"Who are the miners?" he asked.

"Their names are Olmstead and Cahill. Olmstead was on the stage with you at the time of the holdup. He'd been in to Butte for a report on the first few loads, I believe."

"And the drivers? Who do you have on the haul?"

Stroud's eyes narrowed at the questioning but his reply was convincing. "All I can give you is names. None of them were on the regular payroll. We used spare wagons from the Butte station so I had our men pick up a crew to man them. The wagon boss is a bruiser named Noyes. He'd been around these parts and knew the country. As a matter of fact I was the one who put him on a wagon in the first place, mostly to get rid of him. He was hanging around our office in Butte so Lane set him to rounding up a crew."

Hickey had grunted audibly at the name, but Burdick didn't change his calm tone. Quietly as ever he asked, "Can you give us the names of the others?"

"Sure. I just paid the rascals." He pulled a paper from an inner pocket and read them off. "Menendez, Peters, Glamp, Jones, and Ziegler. Noyes also handles a wagon as well as being boss."

"One thing more. Would you remember any of them by nicknames?"

"No—I'm afraid not. I haven't actually seen any except the three I met today. Noyes was one and— Wait a minute! I remember now. They called Menendez Cooky and one of the others was called Squint. Why?"

Burdick was spared a reply. The same freckled urchin who had brought word of the finding of Dolan's body had come bursting in again once more quite breathless.

"Better come quick, Doc," he exploded at Burdick. "Mom's bad."

"What's wrong?"

"Gonna have—a young'un, I reckon— I was goin' fer— Doc Dolan when I found him dead— Come quick, kin yuh? Mom's bad."

"Right away," Burdick assured him. "Lead the way." Over his shoulder he grimaced at the others. "That's the trouble with this town. A man doesn't have anything to keep his mind off his troubles."

It was well along toward midnight when he left the little cottage on the hill and stumbled wearily down the street toward the Burdick house. The past hours had been brutal ones, sapping his dwindling reserves of energy until he had wanted to drop from sheer exhaustion. But he had fought it through, aware that his first real maternity case was one he would never forget. For hours it had been touch-and-go but finally he had known the thrill of triumph, an emotion strong enough to beat back the aching weariness. Now he was leaving behind him an exhausted but grateful mother, a lusty infant, and a thankful group of impressed neighbors. Almost through a fog he realized that he had accomplished something pretty big, something which had given him stature in the minds of those who had watched his fight. It made him forget the other troubles of the basin.

The sun was high when he opened his eyes to find himself sprawled fully dressed on top of his bed. His eyes still burned and his very bones ached but his mind was quickly alert, remembering all the little details of the tangled affairs of the valley. Today he had to find the thinking time he had been needing. If no bank runs developed and no children decided to come into the world perhaps he could work out some details. Of course, he would have to pay a visit to Ned Fishel but he was already planning on that.

He forced himself to deliberation as he shaved, slipping into a fresh flannel shirt before going down to prepare a substantial breakfast. When those details were out of the way he spent a few minutes in copying notes from the records Ellen had assembled. Then he went out.

The morning was fine, sunny but still crisp from the gentle northerly breeze coming down from the high country. There was no scent of smelter dumps in the air, and

Burdick decided that it was a good omen. A little more logically he knew that there wouldn't be any more smelting going on back there in the hills while matters were in such an uproar.

He stopped at Whispering Wilson's stable, ordering a bronc from the toothless hostler who was operating the place in its owner's absence. Then he went on down the street, replying to the greetings of men who had ignored him until now. Apparently last night's chore had sent his stock up a few points. It was heartening but he knew that it wasn't going to help much. Folks might think well of him as a physician but his immediate troubles were along an entirely different line. In some respects it was still a one-man fight.

He found things pretty quiet at the stage line office. It appeared that several businessmen in town were cashing checks as needed and people were beginning to forget their fears. Only one small demand for cash had come into the office all morning.

"Looks like we sent Ellen to Butte on a wild-goose chase," Hickey grumbled.

"Maybe not. When the bank opens there will be people who will get anxious. That's when we'll want plenty of cash on hand."

"I still ain't keen on the idea. There's heap o' risk in haulin' hard cash across the mountains."

"I've been a bit worried on that point. Do you think people know what's up?"

"They likely have guessed."

"Has anyone asked about it?"

"Nobody but Jane Lowry. We hinted that there'd soon be cash to fill out the rest o' the Diamond K payroll."

"Better head out along the trail this afternoon, Tex. I'm going to Fishel's and I'd like to know that somebody is ready to look after things." He didn't say what he meant but it was enough that Hickey understood.

"Mebbe I'll patrol a bit," Tex agreed. "No tellin' when to expect Ellen and Whisper but I'll keep an eye skinned."

It was as much as he could do at the time but Burdick was still worried when he hit the trail upriver.

He found Jane Lowry on duty with the injured man, a hint of trouble showing in place of the humorous glint which generally was in her eyes. Her greeting was cordial, however, and for some time the talk ran only to the business at hand. They changed dressings on Fishel's wounds, noting that the healing process was going along nicely. The nester was even recovered enough to joke, putting in several sly digs about doctors and nurses belonging together.

It was when Burdick was ready to leave that the girl gave him a hint as to what was on her mind. "I'm worried," she said frankly as she followed him out into the yard. "It's Rusty. He acted mighty peculiar after we came back with the payroll money yesterday. He scarcely waited to get back to the ranch with me and then he disappeared."

"Not smart of him," Burdick told her. "Most men would hunt for an excuse to stick around."

"Don't offer me small talk," she warned, her smile brief. "Is there something wrong that Rusty's got himself into?"

He decided to give it to her straight. "There is."

"What?"

"I can't tell you just now. I don't even know the full extent of it. We'll learn it all soon enough, I'm afraid."

She didn't waste time with argument. "I'm afraid I'm pretty muddled. I've learned to distrust the people I thought I trusted most. And some of the folks I didn't trust are turning out to be all right. Why did you lie to me about Dillingham?"

"I didn't."

"But you did. You told me he was a swindler. Yesterday I find him in charge of money. Your money. It doesn't make sense."

Burdick laughed shortly. "Nothing makes sense. Oddly enough, I'm just as muddled as you are. The folks I ex-

pected to find as friends are turning out to be thieves and
I'm depending on strangers or apparent enemies. Your
work here as a nurse is a mild case in point. Dillingham
is another. So is Ellen Davies."

"Did she return from Butte yet?"

"Who said she went?"

"Rusty Aiken. He seemed to pick up the fact somewhere in town."

"Very well. She went—secretly. See what I mean about
not being able to trust friends? There was a leak somewhere."

"Is it important?"

"I hope not—but I'm afraid it is."

He urged his bronc out of the yard, not trusting himself
to say more. At the gate in Fishel's wire he cut north,
angling up the ridge directly toward the mouth of Dog
Robber Gulch. Presently he reached down to get a box
of cartridges from a saddlebag, transferring a handful to
coat pockets. Always he kept his eyes focused on the top
of Hardtack Ridge. There was still the chance that a rifleman might be up there as had been the case before and
he didn't propose to be a sitting duck for anybody.

Actually he didn't expect such a guard to be on duty
today. The gang would be lying low probably, waiting
to see what would happen next. Maybe they only posted
a guard when the mines or the smelter dump was working.
Still it was a relief to enter the gulch without meeting
anyone. Apparently his guesses were working out.

He rode boldly but slowly, taking time to study sign
without actually stopping to do so. There were tracks
aplenty, all of them headed out. A number of riders had
been back into the Reveille Canyon area within the past
day or so but they had gone out again. There was no indication of recent wagon travel. The old ruts were there
but no fresh sign.

As the walls fell away, opening into Reveille Canyon,
he found the first of the prospect holes which had been
so carefully listed on Uncle Jeff's papers. He even con-

sulted the notes he had brought, letting any possible watchers draw their own conclusions. This would be the Little Bonanza, a mine whose name had turned out to be the sheerest optimism. It was one of those owned jointly by the Burdick estate and Sam Kennicott and there was nothing to indicate that it was worth a plugged nickel to either party.

Less than a hundred yards beyond it he spotted the Turkey Neck, closely adjoined by the Sally Em. Prospectors up here must have been pretty chummy, judging by the way they had huddled. Sociable failures, he told himself.

He rounded the turn into the canyon, following the wagon tracks which had passed the three prospect holes without a break. Almost immediately he spotted a shallow depression in the side of the ridge. According to his directions this would be the site of the Blue Monday, the first of the claims owned solely by Jefferson Burdick. This was one of his uncle's pet extravagances, just as the near-by Peter Pan had been a Kennicott folly.

This time Burdick halted to study the place from the saddle. The other claims had been shallow but definite shafts, dug well into the hillsides before the prospectors abandoned hope. The Blue Monday was just a gaping shallow pit. Suddenly he knew what caused it to look that way. A shaft had once been there but it had been caved in.

Suspicion made him study it more closely until he could spot evidences of what had happened. That cave-in had been deliberately accomplished. The rock had not collapsed; someone with tools had broken down the entrance to the tunnel. Why?

He did not delay, remembering the pose he was assuming. Instead he rode on along the floor of the canyon, quickly discovering the secret of all those horse-and-wagon tracks. Traffic had converged on the Peter Pan and one glance at the open tunnel indicated that the mine had been operating with some show of energy.

As he approached, a man came out, cradling a rifle in his arm. It was the dour miner who had ridden the stage from Butte. So far as Burdick could determine the man was alone and apprehensive. Accordingly he waved a careless salute with the paper he still held in his hand.

"Howdy," he greeted. "I'm Frank Burdick. Maybe you remember me from the stage the other day. I'm trying to clear up an estate and it seems there were some mine holdings up this way. Nothing any good, I guess, but I had to take a look. Got any idea where the Turkey Neck or the Blue Monday might be?"

The man frowned, studying Burdick for a long minute before looking away again. When he finally spoke it was with a forced geniality which had an odd air of secret mirth about it. "I reckon yo're in the wrong line o' hills, Burdick. Them old pot holes was over in Reveille Canyon."

"But I thought this was Reveille Canyon," Burdick complained.

"Nope. This is—just another crack in the dad-blamed rocks. No proper name, yo' might say."

"Then how do I find Reveille Canyon? I never rode this country much when I lived in the basin. Too easy to get lost."

The man seemed to be smothering another chuckle. "Yo'll have to go back through Dog—through that gulch back there. Then head straight south about three-four miles till yo' find a rocky draw. About five miles up that you'll find them old diggin's. Not much to find, though."

Burdick shrugged. "Maybe I'll just forget the whole thing. Funny, though; I thought sure I'd hit the right place when I saw the PP on your ore cart. Seemed like this had to be the Peter Pan."

The man started but recovered himself quickly, his swift glance at the burned capitals on the side of the wagon covering his momentary confusion. His laugh was almost real as he explained, "This here's the Pontius Pilate." Then he laughed more loudly as though pleased at his own inventiveness.

"Who's the owner?"

Again there was a hesitation. "Me and a feller named Cahill. So far we ain't struck much but country rock so I reckon we'll soon be movin' on. No point in battin' yer head against a stone wall."

Burdick let it go at that. Offering a few more careless remarks he turned his bronc and rode slowly back along the well-marked trail, studying rock formations as he rode. The thing was beginning to clear up. His guesses had been almost exactly correct.

He was still trying to fit minor pieces to the puzzle when he swung out of Dog Robber Gulch and began to follow the wagon trail toward the northeast. A mile along the trail he noted the hoofprints that came in from the west. Four riders had struck the main trail at that point, apparently some little time after those other men had come out from the canyon country.

The significance of it struck home with a suddenness that was painful. Diamond K men coming to join the canyon gang in a push eastward could mean just one thing. Jane Lowry had not been dreaming when she entertained suspicions about Rusty Aiken's sudden rush to get away from the ranch.

He spurred the bronc into a run, holding the pace until caution warned him that he had to ease off. Haste was essential but nothing could be accomplished by killing the horse. He swung across the end of Hardtack Ridge, getting a brief glimpse of Osage in the distance. Then he was working his way through the rough country, taking a short cut which would permit him to strike the main river trail between Butte and the smaller town. Maybe Tex Hickey would keep his promise and maybe he wouldn't. In either case the enemy was overpowering in numbers—and there was no time to detour into Osage for additional help.

He struck the main trail some six miles north of town, halting immediately to study the confused sign. The rocky ground made clear reading impossible but he came to the conclusion that no substantial body of horsemen had passed this way. Could it be possible that he had misread the whole picture?

· He let his bronc rest while he considered the possibilities but the respite was a short one. A single gunshot sounded from the direction of Osage. It was followed by two others in quick succession, then by a rattle of gunfire which sounded like an impressive skirmish.

"Calamity Rock again!" he exclaimed aloud. "I might have known it!" Instantly he knew what had happened. Expecting the riders to strike at the stage farther east along the trail he had cut to the northeast. It had been a wrong guess, the outlaw concentration coming once more at the Calamity Rock bend. Apparently the stagecoach had arrived quite early—or some other conveyance transporting the cash—and it had passed along the trail before he came down out of the hills. In either case the fat was in the fire.

Stark dread filled him as he sent the tired bronc at a dead run up the riverbank. When all was said and done this was his affair—yet other people were taking the risks for him, standing against that outlaw fire which still rattled briskly along the canyon walls. Then the significance of the shooting eased his mind a shade. The defenders must be doing pretty well to have so much shooting going on. Maybe he could take a hand before it was too late.

Chapter Sixteen

BURDICK WAS SLAMMING HARD down the grade to the Calamity Rock bend when he spotted the two riders ahead of him. For a moment he didn't know whether they were friends or foes but then he saw the handkerchiefs over their faces as they moved out to block his approach. Apparently the outlaws had attacked just beyond the sharp bend in the trail and had sent these two men back on the trail as pickets.

A bullet droned past as the thought came. It was followed by two others, one of them perilously close. By that time Burdick knew that he wasn't going to have any opportunity to think things out. He had to fight his way to Ellen and the others who were keeping up that peppering fire beyond the rock. It was properly his own fight but others were carrying the load for him.

Crouching low along the bronc's neck he drove straight at the outlaw sentries, grimly amused at the panic they were already showing. Neither seemed to have any stomach for meeting this headlong charge, and their shots were going wild as they let their ponies jump around nervously.

He held his fire, ignoring the frantic but poorly-aimed fire, until he was within thirty yards of them. Then he drew fine on the bigger man, pulling back on the reins with his left hand at the same time. The bronc went into a sliding halt, the steadier motion permitting Burdick to aim a little better as he drove in three quick shots. The third slug shoved the outlaw bodily from his saddle, and by that time the other man was wheeling to beat a retreat.

There was no mercy in Frank Burdick now. He shot the outlaw squarely between the shoulder blades, scarcely watching to see the results of the shot. Already he was listening to the sounds of battle beyond the rocky projection.

Shouted orders came faintly to his ears and suddenly he understood the bandit strategy. He also guessed that Tex Hickey had come out from Osage in time to keep that strategy from becoming as deadly effective as it might otherwise have been.

He slid from the saddle, stooping to pick up the gun dropped by the second bandit. Then he was scaling the rugged north side of the promontory known as Calamity Rock. Since the outlaws had permitted their quarry to round the point it seemed certain that members of the gang would be posted on the upper ledges where they could command the road. Both Hickey and the people on the trail would be helpless against such snipers so

Burdick knew that he had to make a flank attack. He would be exposed to fire in getting across but it seemed like the only chance.

He was almost at the crest of the spur when he heard a voice yelling a demand for surrender. A single shot was the only reply. Then the firing died away, and a nearer voice urged companions to close in. Burdick knew a moment of black dread but then he was at the top of the rock, peering down toward the trail where the stagecoach stood motionless. The bandits had used the familiar strategy of shooting a lead horse to anchor the coach.

That part Burdick realized without special thought. For the most part his mind was concerned with two men directly in front of him. One was a rifleman not fifty feet away, a burly fellow who had risen to his knees on a little ledge while he covered the movements of a gunman who was stalking cautiously toward the now silent stagecoach.

"I think I got that last jigger, Ed," the rifleman called. "Yuh kin git on in there now."

The man on the trail looked up in brief acknowledgment and caught sight of Burdick on the sky line. Instantly he yelled the alarm and flung a hasty shot at the newcomer. Burdick heard the slug whine past but he did not offer a reply. It was clear that his greatest danger was from the rifleman just below so he took grim aim as the man swung his weapon around.

For one sickening instant he looked squarely into the bore of the rifle but he refused to let panic spoil his aim. The six-gun bucked against his palm, its roar echoed by the sharper crack of the rifle but the outlaw weapon was swinging far off line when it exploded.

Burdick hesitated only long enough to know that the enemy was down. Then he was over the crest of the rocky ridge, slamming a couple of quick shots at the men in the trail and scrambling for that ledge where the rifleman now lay inert. From somewhere in the near distance another gun boomed, its bullet ricocheting from the rocks above Burdick's head, but he did not pause, looking around only when he had secured the rifle his victim had dropped. One glance told him that the outlaw was quite dead, a second assured him that the rifle was almost fully loaded. Then he concentrated on securing the advantage his surprise attack had gained. Not only was he better armed than he had been but he now held a strategic spot of advantage.

A slug shattered on a rock near him and this time he located the man who had fired it. The fellow was some distance south along the trail, evidently a picket like the others had been back there beyond the rock. Apparently the bandits had distributed their considerable numbers so as to establish a really tight trap. At least it had been planned as a tight one.

Anxiety over the silence around the stagecoach was gnawing at Burdick now but he knew he had a job to do. Before he could undertake any rescue work he had to win a fight. He rested the rifle on the brink of the ledge, waiting breathlessly until he caught another flicker of movement which presaged a shot from the man who had just fired.

The man was careful but Burdick knew his business. Long before he had started the study of medicine he had learned the grim business of gun-fighting. That sort of learning stuck with a man, and now he studied the patch of brush where the movement had appeared. Suddenly it came again, this time directly over the sights of the Winchester. Burdick squeezed the trigger and pulled aside, looking past the muzzle smoke to see a man pitch sideways out of the mesquite.

The diversion had been a matter of seconds only but the fellow on the trail had seized his opportunity, dashing to take cover behind the stagecoach where Burdick did not dare fire at him. By this time several voices were yelling orders from points near by. Now that the moment of surprise was over the bandits were preparing to get rid of this new threat to their project.

Burdick shifted his position a little, trying to prepare

for the attack which would certainly come. It was not a heartening move for it allowed him to see the inert form of Slats McGill on the trail beside the coach. He could only wonder what had happened to the others. Certainly there was no movement to give him any hope that passengers had survived.

Three or four minutes dragged by, as long as that many hours. Then a single shot boomed from upriver and a man yelled, more in alarm than pain. At the same instant another voice from the same general direction started to whoop it up. This time the words were clear.

"Git the broncs! Posse comin' from Osage!"

Instantly lurking outlaws burst into view, all of them heading for the rocky draw which led away from the trail along the south side of the spur. It was the trail along which the earlier band of stage robbers had retreated with their captive. This gang must have picketed their mounts back there in preparation for the ambush. Burdick recognized the thought but had no time to do more than that. Suddenly he was engaged in a brisk gun battle, picking his targets calmly in spite of the storm of lead which the outlaws were aiming at him as they tried to cover their escape. He had the satisfaction of seeing two men go down but then he knew that he had slipped. The man who had taken cover behind the stage suddenly burst into the open with a satchel in his hand. Burdick saw him only for an instant, then the fellow was behind the rocky wall, too close in for Burdick to get a shot at him. The bandits were running but they were taking the loot with them!

Burdick threw all caution to the winds. He swung out over the ledge and scrambled down the steep rocky wall, almost oblivious to the rattle of gunfire which was enveloping the trail to his left. It was only when the tide of battle swung back past the spur that he knew what was happening. The bandits were in full retreat toward the mountains, pursued by those newcomers from Osage.

In the same detached fashion he knew that the outlaws had managed to snatch the bank money in a final desperate gamble but for the moment he was not concerned. All that mattered was the silent stagecoach below him. What had happened to its occupants?

He landed sprawling on the trail, leaving the captured Winchester where he dropped it as he ran toward the coach. A glance told him that Slats McGill was dead, two bloody holes showing in the small of his thin back. Then he was staring at the huddle of bodies inside the riddled Concord.

A noise behind him made him wheel, but it was Tex Hickey and Charley Bigelow. He wondered briefly what the nester was doing here but his only comment was a brief order. "Help me with these people," he said.

They lifted out the body of a big, unshaven man who had been shot squarely between the eyes. Burdick let the others handle the inert weight, turning back with a flicker of hope as he saw an arm move. Dusk was falling rapidly now but there was light enough for him to see that two people had been pinned beneath the dead man—and both of them were moving!

"Git me outa here!" Whispering Wilson's sibilant tones urged. "This gal is hurt, and I ain't doin' her no good crushin' her like this!"

Quick hands gave the required assistance, and the liveryman was soon on his feet, swaying a little as he clutched a limp arm but apparently not too badly injured. By that time Burdick was bending over the twisted huddle that was Ellen Davies.

He waved Hickey aside. "Don't move her until I see if there are any bones broken."

Bigelow had gone around to the far side of the Concord, opening the door so that more light came into the vehicle. It was enough to show Burdick a large red stain at the side of the dusty jacket the girl was wearing. The opened door permitted her to stretch cramped legs and he saw that she was capable of movement even though she did not open her eyes. That helped.

Swift examination disclosed that there was only one

injury, a gunshot wound which had raked across her left side some six inches below the armpit. With his jackknife he slit the bloody garments, exposing the furrow which had caused considerable loss of blood but which must have missed the ribs. Then he nodded to Hickey. "We'll slide her out. Easy, now."

She moaned softly as they moved her to the ground, opening her eyes for a moment as Burdick bent over her. "You—" she murmured. "You—"

"Quiet. We'll fix you up in a jiffy but save your strength."

He had to steel himself to the work before him, raging inwardly because his hands wanted to tremble. As a physician he knew that this was not a bad wound, that the worst part was the way she had lost blood while waiting for help. But it was hard to keep thinking as a doctor. He was too conscious of unprofessional factors, too conscious of the stark fear which had come upon him at realization of her danger.

Hickey was not idle during those moments. Breaking into the boot he came up with a neat trunk, rifling it of clean garments which could be torn into bandages. Then he went for water at the mountain brook which rippled down past Calamity Rock into the Big Hole River.

Burdick accepted the assistance without comment, aware that other men were moving around in the gathering gloom. He completed his work with dispatch and picked up a coat from the coach to wrap around the girl. "Let her rest awhile," he directed, voice steady again. "Where's Wilson?"

"Here," the liveryman husked. "Reckon I got me a busted arm but it'll keep. See if anybody else need yo' wuss'n I do."

More men were returning all the time, evidently having given up the pursuit of the bandits, but no one mentioned an injury. So Burdick turned his attention to Wilson, this time working with the calm skill of the trained surgeon. Someone produced a lantern, and he was soon able to determine that Wilson's arm was not too serious. The small bone had been broken by the slug and would need careful attention but for the present it was a simple matter of protective first aid. While he took care of it Wilson told his story, the surrounding silence almost painful as men strained their ears to catch the whispered words.

"We'd just got around the rock when they plugged a lead hoss. Mebbe they figgered we wouldn't put up no fight but we fooled 'em. Bender—that's the gent Ellen hired for a guard in Butte—cut loose at a jigger along the trail and I heard Slats McGill fire a shot or two. Then it sounded like a whole army was shootin'. Ellen got hit almost at the first fire and I shoved her down to the bottom o' the coach. We beat off the fust rush and then somebody started bangin' away upriver."

"Me," Hickey explained. "I was comin' along the trail when I heard the openin' shots. I busted right into a couple o' rannies what seemed to be on guard around the bend. I had to take cover and we done some right fancy dodgin' while I was tryin' to work my way around 'em." There was a bloodstain on the lawman's upper arm but he was carrying his gun in that hand so Burdick knew that the wound must be unimportant.

"They rushed in again," Wilson said, "after holdin' up fer the other fracas. This time I didn't hear any shots from McGill. There was a jigger up on the rocks and we couldn't tell where the polecat was hidin'. He had a rifle and he made it mighty hot while the other jiggers closed in on us."

"I heard it," Hickey growled, "but I couldn't git on the scene in time."

"Anyway, I got one in the arm and fell over on the gal. About that time Bender got knocked over hard. He fell on top o' me and I figgered the jig was up. Seemed like I didn't have my proper wits fer a spell and when I started to think straight I heard Doc's voice. Sounded right good, I wanta say!"

Burdick straightened up from his work. "Try to keep

from moving that arm until we get into town and treat it properly. Any more wounded?" He looked squarely at Hickey.

The lawman glanced down at the red place on his shirt, then grinned at Burdick. "Nicked," he said tersely, raising the arm to show that he could still use it. "Anybody else stop a slug?"

A pair of grim men dragged a prisoner forward. The fellow's handkerchief mask had fallen around his neck and he was dragging a leg that was bloody from knee to boot top.

"No use fixin' him up, Doc," someone called. "Gonna hang him anyway."

"Red Worrell!" Hickey exclaimed.

Burdick remembered the name. "Fine," he said, quietly triumphant. "He ought to be just the man we need. Close enough to the leaders to know a few things and unimportant enough so we can afford to swap him his life for a bit of talk."

"Don't bank on it!" the redheaded one snarled defiantly. "I ain't talkin'."

"Get him over there where I can look at his leg," Burdick ordered. "He might change his mind when he finds out how little talking he needs to do."

The lantern threw its dull gleam on the circle of tense faces as Burdick started to work, talking at the same time for the benefit of the men around him as well as for the ears of the groaning bandit.

"It was quite a gang you'd thrown together, Worrell. At first I couldn't believe the evidence when it pointed to so many men being involved. Then I began to see what had happened. At least three different gangs of outlaws had been thrown together and were acting as allies—no doubt waiting for the chance to cut each others' throats. I suppose your boss was Rusty Aiken, eh?"

Worrell did not reply, merely gritting his teeth while men held him down for the surgical treatment Burdick was giving him.

"It doesn't make much difference. The point is that Aiken had a scheme to get control of the Big Hole Basin. He saw that the nesters had the right idea when they planned to concentrate on blooded cattle, figuring on the superior qualities of Montana bunch grass to produce high-priced beef. What he wanted to do was to spread that idea to the whole basin—but not for Lowry. He figured to grab it all for himself so he hired a couple of thugs like you to stir up a range war. The nesters and Lowry were supposed to get so sick of gunplay that both sides would give up. Then Aiken would buy them both out for a song—provided he couldn't find a way to steal everything outright."

He was silent for a moment as he concentrated on surgery, then continued. "But Aiken blundered into something almost as big—and just as dirty. He found that a prospector named Olmstead—or maybe it was Cahill—had struck a new lode of pay dirt in an abandoned mine back in the canyons. It looked mighty good but it was somebody else's property. So they figured to work it on the quiet, trying to find out how good it really was. They got a bit of backing and hauled a few loads of refractory ore back into the mountains where they set up a sort of open-dump smelter. Roasting the ore with salt works pretty well. It drives off the sulphur and arsenic, turning the silver into chloride so it can be recovered and leaving the copper in a condition to be handled at a profit. By using the process the bootleg miners could make it profitable to haul their loot away in partly refined form. It wouldn't have been worth while to run a few wagons of ore out but this way they could make a profit while they were trying to decide which way the seam of paydirt was running."

He reached for bandages and spoke directly to Hickey for a moment. "The place is Reveille Canyon, Tex. You almost stumbled on it when you were hunting Dillingham but you just missed. Maybe you'll find it a good idea to take a posse out there in the morning. Some of those

scared bandits might try to hole up at their old headquarters."

"But what's the connection between Aiken and the mine
game?" Hickey wanted to know.

"I'm guessing Aiken forced his way in. He probably
stumbled on the other deal and guessed that it might be
a good thing to watch. He had a crew of gunnies like Red
here. It wouldn't have been hard for him to persuade the
other crew that they needed those guns with 'em rather
than against 'em. Meanwhile the mine outfit had made a
deal for wagons with drivers who didn't report back to
the company office. Those drivers composed the rest of the
gang." He paused a moment before adding, "I think most
of the crowd was here today, ganged up in a desperate
attempt to confuse the whole situation and at the same
time grab a big chunk of money."

"Which part they done." Hickey's growl was almost
vicious. "Too bad that polecat with the valise got clean
away."

"It was just money," Burdick shrugged. "We'll survive.
Now let's get these people on the road to Osage. I can't
do any more for them here." If he sounded unconcerned
about the loss of the cash it was because he felt exactly that
way. Finding Ellen no more seriously injured than she was
had relieved him of such a load of worry that he couldn't
find time now for any regrets.

Chapter Seventeen

IT REQUIRED SOME LITTLE TIME to get started for Osage.
The wounded had to be loaded as comfortably as possible,
and Burdick saw to it that Ellen was given the choice position. Meanwhile the men who had arrived so oppor-
tunely were getting the dead horse out of the traces and
replacing him with one of the outlaw broncs which had
been abandoned in the gulch. Finally all was in readiness
and the stage moved forward, an Osage driver handling
it gingerly both for the sake of the injured and because

one of the front wheels had lost a couple of spokes in the gun battle.

Burdick had tried to keep his mind on his duties as a physician while all this was happening but all around him excited men were talking, asking questions and offering their own theories. Gradually he learned several things. One was that Jane Lowry was responsible for the relief expedition. She had galloped into Osage late in the afternoon, accompanied by three nesters, and shouting the word that there was a plot on foot to attack the stage. No one seemed to know how she had come by the information and no one seemed to care. It was enough that she had been right. The only regret was that she had not brought the warning sooner. The bandits had suffered heavy losses but they had killed two good men and they had gone away with the money.

The slow journey to town gave Hickey a chance to talk with Burdick, and plans were made as swiftly as possible. One party was to return at dawn to search the scene of the flight for outlaw bodies and for any clues which might turn up. Another force was to strike for Reveille Canyon, hopeful that the retreating bandits would hole up there for a division of the loot. It didn't seem likely that they would remain in the basin very long; they must know that the game was ended for all of them.

Osage turned out en masse to meet the little cavalcade as it limped into town. Advance riders had told the story in part, and someone had been smart enough to open Doc Dolan's empty house as an emergency hospital. Burdick recognized the wisdom of the move as soon as they were directed to the building and was quite prepared to find Jane Lowry in charge there. The girl had broken open the closet and was setting the place in order for the work that was to be done.

He commended her with a brief: "Nice thinking," and started with his own preparations. Volunteer helpers brought the three patients in, leaving two armed men with the wounded bandit. Then the other men disappeared, evidently willing to leave this part of the show to Doctor Burdick.

It was astonishing how many needs had been anticipated. Jane Lowry and an older woman who had helped with the maternity case took over as nurses while several others hovered in the background, providing help and materials as needed. Burdick knew a sense of gratitude and appreciation even though he scarcely had time to say so. Still they seemed to understand each other, and the work went forward swiftly.

Eventually it was over. Ellen was tucked into bed on a cot in the front room, properly bandaged and beginning to recover some of her spirits. Whispering Wilson was on Dolan's bed, grumbling at being made to stay there even though his face was still haggard and drawn from the ordeal he had gone through. The bandit had been given equally good treatment and had been hauled away to the calaboose, still under guard. Only then did Burdick look around at the tense but excited faces about him. "You're great people," he said simply. "Thanks."

Shaking off their half-embarrassed congratulations he went through into the front room where Jane Lowry was persuading Ellen to take a little broth. His eyes were only for Ellen as he asked, "Feeling better?"

"Physically, yes—but it hurts to know they got the money."

"Forget the money!"

She grimaced tiredly. "But it hurts my pride. I thought I was so smart when I made up that dummy satchel."

He stared as the meaning of her words struck home. "You what?"

"I made believe that the money was in a satchel. Even Wilson didn't know. Actually the satchel had rocks and paper in it. The money was in the trunk in the boot."

He grinned, shaking his head in wonder. "I might have known you'd do something smart like that. I'd better go find Hickey before he sends a lot of tired men on a wild-goose chase. Take charge here, will you, Jane?"

He found a dozen men at Hickey's office getting instructions from the lawman. They were grim and determined but their questions were anxious as they greeted him with questions about the injured.

"Everything fine," he told them. "Even better than we thought. Ellen tells me the money was not in the valise but in one of the trunks in the boot. We'd better—"

He didn't have time to finish. Men were rushing across toward the stage station where the stage had already been unloaded. Dillingham and Stroud were there, surrounded by a half-dozen men who seemed to have been giving Stroud a pretty uncomfortable time. The stage line manager's red face had lost some of its usual color and he was protesting that he had known nothing of the true nature of the business for which the freight wagons had been rented.

Burdick looked at the pile of baggage which had been dumped in the office. There were only two trunks, one of them the opened one which had been despoiled for emergency dressings. The other was a battered old box tied with rope, now being used by Dillingham as a seat.

"Climb off a minute," Burdick said quietly. "I want to see what's in that thing."

He slashed at the ropes while some men watched in wonder and the others, gloating over superior knowledge, waited for him to throw the lid back. The trunk did not even have a lock and when the last cord was cut he flipped it open to disclose neatly packed bundles of currency and the familiar sacks in which hard money was usually handled. There was a roar of triumph, and Burdick let his smile have its way. There hadn't been much to smile about in the past week so it seemed like a good time for one.

"Get the safe open, Virgil," he directed. "Miss Davies was smart enough to save the money; we won't risk it in the open."

"Hold up a bit," Dillingham interrupted. "I figure you'd better stash that tin right in the bank."

"But the bank is—"

"Sure it's locked—but I can unlock it." He produced a key and a tiny slip of paper. "I found this in Whiteside's room the other mornin' but it didn't seem like a good time to tell you about it. Folks mighta been unreasonable if the bank was open and it seemed like they'd play along better if they knew we were going to some kind of trouble to keep the town goin'." He grinned amiably at the astonished men around him. "That's right, ain't it, gents? You wouldn't rush this office but you'd have got real panicky about gettin' your tin outa the bank."

The impudence of it caught their fancy. Men swore and laughed by turns while Dillingham managed a still-painful wink at Burdick. Then they lashed the rickety trunk together again and started a boisterous parade to the bank. Burdick was content to have them make a celebration of it. They were celebrating a triumph for him and they had earned it. Most of them had completely forgotten their earlier hostility.

Dillingham made quite a ceremony of opening the bank and the safe, his patter drawing hoots of delight as the cash was tucked away. Then he turned to hand keys and combination to Burdick. "Take 'em, Doc," he said. "I reckon I've had my fling."

Burdick pushed them back. "You're in charge here," he said shortly. "Osage needs a banker. I think you can handle it. I hope you'll find it more profitable than peddling tonic."

For an instant Dillingham was stopped, at a loss for words. Then he recovered and blurted, "Thanks, Doc. I won't let you down."

The babble of approval was cut short by two quick shots from outside. Instantly men were fighting to get out, someone at the door bawling indistinctly about a jail break.

"Stay here!" Burdick snapped at the new banker. "Lock up and stay locked!"

Three more shots, unevenly spaced, rang out as he tried to get through the shoving mob at the door. Finally he was out in the darkness, part of a crowd that was streaming toward the calaboose. Quickly he found himself in a ring of muttering men which surrounded two figures, a bulky one prone on the ground and a lanky man who stood nervously over the other one, a gun dangling in nervous fingers.

"It's Sam Kennicott!" a man squeaked, nerves doing tricks with his voice. "Shot in the back. Who done it, Moon?" Burdick saw then that the other fellow was Deputy Sheriff Moon Peckham. He shoved forward then and saw that Tex Hickey had done the same thing.

"I shot him," Peckham stated flatly. "I didn't know who he was."

There was a swift mutter of anger and armed men pushed in to menace the deputy. They had seen enough violence for one night without having the mayor shot down like this. And Peckham's story sounded pretty thin.

Burdick intervened hastily, shoving Hickey across so that he could protect Peckham from the other side. "Hold it, everybody," he shouted. "Let me see if I can do anything for Kennicott." Then in a lower voice: "Talk fast, Moon. Tell 'em what happened."

It didn't take many seconds to see that the two bullet holes in Kennicott's back had killed him instantly. Meanwhile Peckham's story was coming out, the crowd listening in an ugly mood.

"I didn't go along to the bank with the rest of yuh," Peckham said, "because I spotted somebody sneakin' along past the backs o' the houses. Things bein' what they was I decided to watch so I seen this jasper slide into the alley where we're standin'. I closed in a mite and heard him call to the jigger inside the calaboose. I figgered it was a jail break but as I started to take a hand the outside man fired two shots through the window and started to run. I went after him and yelled for him to stop. He cut a shot at me so I let him have it. I didn't even know who he was till I stooped over him."

Hickey roared down the murmur of disbelief. "Moon,

lemme look at yuhr gun. Doc, better check the iron Sam
was totin'. It's there on the ground. Somebody else see
what's happened to Red Worrell."

Even the most skeptical soon knew that Deputy Peckham had told the truth. His gun contained two empties.
Kennicott's weapon had been fired three times. Red Worrell was dead at a side window of the jail, killed by two
shots which had hit him in the chest from powder-burn
range.

"Better go to your office and thresh out details," Burdick
said tiredly. "These men have a right to know all we can
tell them."

Hickey shook his head. "Not in my place," he said
dryly. "We got some dead outlaws lined up there. Includin'
Noyes and Aiken. Rusty was the gent on the ledge, in
case yuh didn't know. Noyes was in the brush across the
trail. Them two make it certain yuh had the right idea.
Both Diamond K riders and Noyes's wagon bullies was
mixed up in the deal."

They finally set up their meeting in the Burdick house,
reminding many of them of the recent session in which
Mayor Kennicott had played the rather bombastic judge.
Doctor Burdick remarked on the fact, glancing around at
the grimly expectant faces.

"I guess I was sure of Kennicott then," he told them.
"He was too anxious to tie up the Whiteside affair with
the shooting of my uncle. If he could make us think
Whiteside guilty of the murder it would take the pressure
off and keep me from looking further.

"But I didn't believe Whiteside was guilty. I still don't.
He had been gambling with bank money and he went
crazy at fear of getting caught but I don't think he even
suspected this other crookedness in the basin. Maybe some
of you didn't know it but I had just one idea in mind
when I started sifting this job. I was out to catch the murderer of my uncle. I stumbled on the rest incidentally but
always I was thinking of that murderer. I wanted to find
some rat who had been hard pressed for time, somebody

so desperate he couldn't wait for a dying man to die.

"Whiteside didn't fit that requirement. Probably he could have covered up for a long time. Maybe he could have replaced his borrowings before an accounting could be made. To Whiteside the death of Jefferson Burdick was a real blow because it hastened the day when an executor would look at the bank's records. Whiteside didn't want my uncle to die."

Nods of understanding greeted the logic of it, and he went on a little more easily. "Virgil Stroud was another suspect. I knew that he was the man who had tampered with the mails in an effort to keep me from returning to Osage. He was up to something crooked, all right, but he didn't fit the description of a man driven to frantic murder.

"Investigation bore that out. Stroud's books were in good order. He was making good money. He had nothing to gain by my uncle's death. All that mattered to him was that I should stay away from here until a certain date. He tried to keep me away—and he wasn't careful how many thugs helped him with the project—but he didn't kill my uncle."

"Then yuh got nothin' on Stroud?" Hickey seemed disappointed.

"Sure I have. He has been interfering with the delivery of United States mail. That part I think I can prove. I believe, but can't prove, that he had watchers in Butte with instructions to stop me. Noyes was one of them. Maybe Stroud didn't know that Noyes was also playing a couple of other angles but there was an understanding between them, I'm certain."

He broke off with an impatient gesture. "But Stroud's not important. It was the Reveille Canyon setup that made me see Sam Kennicott in the show. I was trying to link Sam with the deal when I asked some of you about salt shipment. I knew that open smelting of ores required salt and I thought Kennicott might have brought it in, pretending that it was for his hotel. That hauling contract threw me off. The chartered freight wagons took out partly refined ores and brought in salt without any of it showing on the local books.

"Actually I never did get proof against Sam. His own guilty conscience was his undoing when he tried to dispose of Red Worrell before the fellow could do any talking. However, I think I know the main facts. Somehow or other a new vein of ore was discovered in the old workings of the Peter Pan and Blue Monday mines. Kennicott knew about it and believed that the lode apexed in the Blue Monday. According to mining law he was on the outside. Uncle Jeff owned the Blue Monday and could claim everything.

"Kennicott decided to double-cross his friend. He had the Blue Monday sealed off and proceeded to work the Peter Pan secretly, trying to get out the ore before anyone would know about the discovery. Somehow Uncle Jeff became suspicious. His health was too bad for him to ride out there so he hired a stranger named Noyes to investigate. Noyes apparently saw what was going on but he didn't report it all to Uncle Jeff. Instead he tried to blackmail Sam Kennicott. Sam paid him to get out of town and keep quiet but Noyes was hired on the hauling job by Virgil Stroud and got right back into the picture, in time to join forces with Rusty Aiken and his gunnies.

"Kennicott must have been pretty worried after he paid Noyes to go away. Sam was mighty proud of his position in the community and he knew that word of what he had done would ruin him. It wasn't so much that he had actually stolen ore from another man's mine; it was the obvious fact that he had deliberately schemed to cheat a friend, a friend who had backed him in his election. He knew that Uncle Jeff suspected. Otherwise Noyes wouldn't have been hired. So he decided to kill my uncle before any exposure could take place. He did."

There was a clearing of throats as men recognized the emotion which had come into his voice, but Burdick went on hurriedly. "After that it got complicated. Rusty Aiken declared himself in, and Kennicott was probably willing.

It helped to confuse the issue and gave Sam a chance to appear as an injured party, a mine owner whose property was being looted. It seems likely that no one but Cahill or Olmstead, the prospectors, knew of Sam's real part—but Sam couldn't be certain on that point. That's why he had to kill Red Worrell."

It took a long time to clear up minor details so that everyone understood the whole miserable plot. By that time it was daylight, and Burdick crawled wearily into bed, exhausted in both mind and body. It was just past noon when he opened his eyes again.

Instantly contrite at his neglect of the patients at Dolan's he dressed hurriedly, shaved, and started across toward the old medico's forlorn building. It was something of a surprise to find the town looking so normal. People were going about their various errands in quiet fashion, almost as though the past night had not been one of violence and tragedy. Even the bank seemed to be open for business. Evidently Lum Dillingham had taken his commission seriously.

Several people greeted Burdick as he hurried across toward Dolan's, their smiles cordial. It did something for him. These folks were speaking to a man they had come to like and admire. He knew it and was a little proud.

He found Sheriff Hickey and Jane Lowry with Ellen and Whispering Wilson. The patients looked better than the red-eyed Miss Lowry and the weary-looking lawman.

"Both invalids doing fine," Miss Lowry reported with mock formality. "They're already getting spoiled so don't give them too much attention."

"That's right," Ellen agreed, offering a smile that made Burdick feel pretty good. "Right now we're mostly victims of curiosity. Sheriff Hickey has been giving us a treatment but you'll have to do the rest."

It seemed obvious that medical treatment was not immediately needed for either patient so Burdick sat down on the foot of Ellen's cot, studying her intently for a moment before turning to Hickey with a curt: "Anything new?"

"Not enough to wake yuh up fer," Hickey grumbled. "I had a posse in Dog Robber Gulch at daybreak. No trace o' the stage bandits but we picked up Olmstead and Cahill. They tell a purty straight yarn and it fits with what yuh figgered last night. It was Cahill found the lode in the Blue Monday. They was honest with Sam Kennicott and thought they was runnin' everything on the level. They figgered the hush-hush part was nacheral caution."

Burdick recalled the way Olmstead had lied to him but he shrugged it off. "Might as well let 'em go. They weren't important."

"Suits me. But I ain't keen on lettin' Stroud git away. He ducked out durin' the night with the cash outa the stage line safe. I got men on his trail."

"Forget him. There wasn't much cash on hand after you and Dillingham got through playing bankers. Virgil had that much coming to him and I don't think I want to prosecute. Actually he'll be hard to replace in the job."

He turned to stare thoughtfully at Ellen, noting the color that came into her cheeks before the scrutiny. "Wonder how your father would like that job, Ellen?" he asked. "He could tinker with guns between busy periods. Do you think you could persuade him to handle it for me? Same deal as Stroud had."

"I'm sure he will," she replied. "And thanks for the offer."

Hickey cut in again. "Peckham brung in two more dead outlaws from Calamity Rock. Seems like yuh done some right smart shootin' out there."

Suddenly Burdick remembered Rusty Aiken. Rusty had supposedly been betrothed to Jane Lowry. For a moment he hated to look toward the girl, knowing that Hickey's remark must have opened the still-fresh wound.

It was Jane's voice that broke the silence. "Don't worry about me," she said, a trace of flippancy hiding the hurt. "I understand."

He smiled his relief. "I wanted to ask you about that.

You did seem to understand when no one else did. How come you got that help on the way?"

Again he had a feeling that she was putting on an act, pretending some of her old pertness to cover a hurt that still was there. "Remember what I told you that first evening you were in town—that I'm a smart girl? That's it—I figure things out. Lately I'd begun to distrust Rusty Aiken. I had a feeling that he was stirring up trouble when he should have been trying to prevent it. Yesterday he was restless, nervous when we left town with the payroll. Several times he mentioned the extra cash that was supposed to be on its way and I knew he was thinking hard about it, trying to figure when it would come and along what trail. He left me as soon as we reached home, and I knew he was riding back into the mountains. I told you about it at Fishel's and I saw that the information bothered you. So I put two and two together. Rusty was planning a stage robbery."

"You'd have been pretty embarrassed if you'd guessed wrong," Burdick commented.

"I suppose so. But I wasn't long in doubt. I stopped at the Bigelows' for help and promptly got an earful. They'd been suspecting the worst of Aiken for a long time, realizing that he was the one back of the trouble between the nesters and us."

"Smart work," Burdick told her. "You've got quite a head on you."

"Just good eyes," she retorted. "For example, I observed the way you have been looking at our lady patient. Don't tell me I'm wrong when I believe there is more than professional concern behind your glances!"

He looked toward Ellen long enough to see another rush of color. Then he said quietly, "You're not wrong."

Miss Lowry stood up briskly, reaching for her hat. "Of course not. Now I'm going off duty long enough to talk business with some gentlemen at the bank." Almost too casually she added, over her shoulder, "That man Dillingham is certainly full of ideas. Almost before the sound of shooting died away he was promoting a stock raisers' association for this basin. The idea is to pool resources and work for improved breeds. Charley Bigelow just stopped in to ask me to attend a little meeting on the subject. He's impressed with the idea and it sounds pretty good to me."

Burdick swallowed his astonishment. "Better pick up Mark Clay and take him along with you," he advised. "You'll need a lawyer to protect you against that Dillingham. Otherwise we'll have you tight in the clutches of the bank."

She turned to give him a broad wink. "Get Clay for yourself," she fired back. "You'll need him to protect the bank's interest when I get through with Dillingham."

Hickey scratched his whiskers thoughtfully as the girl went out. "Yuh know, Frank, I think she likes that crazy coot."

Burdick was still fighting surprise but he managed to chuckle. "Maybe he's not so crazy. Sounds to me like he's found what he wanted and he's making a fast play to hold on to it."

"What d'yuh mean? The bank or the gal?"

"Maybe both. I hope so."

"Will you leave him in charge of the bank?" Ellen interrupted.

He looked down at her, the corners of his mouth quirked slightly. "I never make any but medical decisions without consulting my chief adviser," he said solemnly. "What's the advice?"

For a moment she seemed to be studying him. Then she replied, "I think he has earned the chance. Certainly the town likes his style."

"Then we've got that point settled. Dillingham runs the bank and Bob Davies takes over the stage line."

"And I'll help him," Ellen said softly, "after you go away."

Burdick came slowly to his feet, partly turning to face Hickey and Wilson. "Gents," he announced, drawling a little, "I'm fixin' to make a speech. It won't be long but it'll be important—to me. About a week ago I had some mighty fancy ideas about settin' up as a doctor in a big town where maybe I'd get to be famous or something. I've kinda changed my mind. Somehow I've come to the conclusion that what a man needs most is to get himself fitted into a spot where he likes his neighbors and where his neighbors like him. Osage needs somebody to fill Doc Dolan's shoes. I'm nominating me." He turned back to Ellen. "How about that nomination, adviser? What's your vote on that one?"

The girl turned her head to look at Hickey. "Sheriff," she said clearly, "will you escort Mr. Wilson into the next room? I'd like to register this vote as a secret ballot."

Hickey's whiskers parted in a wide grin. He helped Wilson to his feet and the pair of them started toward the kitchen. At the door it was Wilson who turned to look back at the scene they were leaving. His voice was appropriately confidential as he muttered, "Some secret!"